M
HOLLYWOOD HEARTS 4

Jean C. Joachim

Mainstream Romance

Secret Cravings Publishing

www.secretcravingspublishing.com

A Secret Cravings Publishing Book
Mainstream Romance

Movie Lovers
Copyright © 2013 Jean C. Joachim
Print ISBN: 978-1-61885-901-3

First E-book Publication: June 2013
First Print Publication: September 2013

Cover design by Dawné Dominique
Edited by Tabitha Bower
Proofread by Carolyn Gibbs
All cover art and logo copyright © 2013 by Secret Cravings Publishing

ALL RIGHTS RESERVED: This literary work may not be reproduced or transmitted in any form or by any means, including electronic or photographic reproduction, in whole or in part, without express written permission.

All characters and events in this book are fictitious. Any resemblance to actual persons living or dead is strictly coincidental.

PUBLISHER
Secret Cravings Publishing
www.secretcravingspublishing.com

DEDICATION

To Ruth Joachim, my beloved mother-in-law.

Acknowledgments

I'd like to thank the following for their help and support: Larry Joachim, Tabitha Bower, my editor, Sandy Sullivan, my publisher, Marilyn Reisse Lee, my Book Buddies, friends and readers who make writing books so worthwhile.

MOVIE LOVERS
HOLLYWOODS HEARTS 4

Jean C. Joachim

Copyright © 2013

Chapter One

Grace Brewster couldn't control her breathing. *Alone with Gunther Quill. Little me with one of the biggest producers in Hollywood.* He leaned against the corner of his desk. The sleeves of his white shirt were rolled up to the elbows, the neck, unbuttoned. His light blue striped tie hung loose. Grace noticed his perfect haircut and the whitest smile she'd ever seen. Brown hair going gorgeously gray at the temples and broad shoulders drew her attention.

No wedding ring. No family pictures on his desk or credenza. He's sex on wheels.

His dark brown eyes feasted on her body, not missing one curve or her dangerously low-cut top. Suddenly feeling naked, Grace leaned back a little in her chair, folding her arms across her breasts. Her rich brown curls fell loosely about her shoulders. She blinked at him with the same big, ocean blues as her sister, famous actress Cara Brewster.

"Tell me a little about your script, Ms. Brewster. Does it have a love scene?"

She gulped, her mouth dry as day-old bread. "Of course."

"Tell me…no, no. Show me." His eyes danced as he strolled closer to her.

"Show you?" Her palms began to sweat as she rose slowly from her chair. "How?"

"The best scriptwriters act out their scripts. Show me. Make me feel it." His magnetic gaze held hers.

Before she could catch her breath, he was standing right in front of her, his chest almost touching hers. He reached out to her locks, rubbing some fine strands between his fingers. "You are just as beautiful as your sister," he whispered.

Grace stepped back. "Thank you, Mr. Quill. That's quite a compliment."

"Gunther. Now show me, Grace. Does your heroine have passion for the hero?"

She nodded.

"How does she show it?"

"Well…she…uh…she…" She looked around the room, avoiding his face.

"Does he do this?" He leaned over and placed his lips on hers, snaking his arm around her waist. Grace's pulse kicked into high gear. The warmth of his kiss aroused her, but fear fought with desire. *He's a producer. What are you doing? You don't even know him. This is business.* She placed her hands on his chest and pushed. But he was like steel and didn't budge.

Bending down, he whispered in her ear, "Does he make love to her?" His mouth was on her neck while he pulled her closer.

"Mr. Quill…"

"Gunther…"

"Okay. Gunther…this is about my script, right? This is business."

"Of course it is. We're only acting out your script. Show me how she makes love to him. Make it real. I need to feel it for the audience to feel it."

"Shouldn't I be doing that with words?"

"Movies are pictures, Grace, my dear. Action, images, are more important than words."

"But…" Her heart beat wildly.

"Show me," he repeated, sliding his fingers up over her breast.

This time she shoved harder. "Wait a minute…" she began, but words stuck in her throat.

He stepped back and dropped his hand. The fire in his eyes turned to ice.

"Do you want me to read your script? Do you know how many get dropped on my door every day? Hundreds. What makes yours special? I need to know you have the passion to write a convincing love scene."

She stared at her fingernails.

"Grace. If you can't convince me, how the hell are you going to convince an audience?"

"But I thought..."

"Don't waste my time. My secretary has your treatment and script?" He moved back to rest against his desk.

She nodded. "You want me to read it, don't you?" She swallowed. "Make me want to read it. Show me your script is hotter, smarter, better than the other five hundred waiting for me. *Convince* me to read it." His gaze warmed. She raised her chin to meet his stare. Lust glittered in his eyes.

"You want me to believe you come in here dressed like that, but you had no intention of seducing me?"

A moment of clarity burst through the confusion in her mind. If she wanted him to read her script, she was expected to have sex with him. A sense of calm washed over her when she figured out what was happening. *Am I that desperate? He's sexy. I could do worse. If he reads it and likes it, I'm in.*

A war raged inside her. This script was everything to her as she struggled to find her way as a writer in a cutthroat business, where her sister was a queen and she was non-existent. But to prostitute herself for it was over the top. *It's not like he's married. Maybe like a hook-up? I don't do hook-ups.*

The phone on his desk buzzed. Gunther leaned over to pick it up. "No, no. Hold all my calls." He replaced the receiver and turned his attention back to Grace. Like a snake who has hypnotized his prey, Gunther slithered across the open space between them. Testing the waters, he ran his finger down her face. "Such beauty should not go...untasted."

"My script. My story. It's about a girl named Jackie and a guy name Brad..." The words came out in a rush.

"Tell me all, my lovely," he said as he drew her near. His lips caressed her neck while his hand slid the shoulder of her blouse down, exposing her breast to his gaze.

* * * *

With a shaking hand, Grace turned the key in the ignition of her SUV. *What just happened?* She put her head down on the steering wheel as the motor purred quietly. *You slept with Gunther*

Quill. Idiot! You let him use you. A wave of nausea flashed through her belly as she jammed the car into drive and pulled out of the parking lot.

When she arrived at the dance studio for her class, Grace raced into the ladies room to throw up. Breathing heavy, she washed her face and mouth. Weakness washed through her body.

As she leaned against the bathroom wall, cooling her hot forehead against the tile, her instructor, Dorrie Rogers, pushed open the door. "Grace! Are you okay?"

She nodded.

"You're pale as a ghost. What happened?"

"Nothing, Dorrie, nothing. I'm fine." Grace pushed away to stand on her own as blood rushed back to her face, and her legs began to feel steady again.

Dorrie put an arm around her friend. "Hey, you don't have to come to class today. We'll extend your lessons."

"I'm fine. I want to dance." She applied lipstick with a trembling hand.

"Don't bullshit me, you're not fine."

Two other students entered, eliminating Dorrie and Grace's privacy.

"I want to dance. It'd be good for me."

"We'll see," Dorrie said as she pulled out a comb and ran it through her auburn hair.

"Meet you inside," Grace said, pushing through the door. She entered the large, sunny room with the shiny, light wood floor. The mirrored wall shouted her image back at her so she could see how bad she looked. Grace put down her bag and gripped the barre. She started slowly, stretching and bending.

Dorrie and the other women gathered and joined Grace in warm-up exercises. Grace directed her focus on dancing, trying not to think about what had just happened in Gunther Quill's office. The smirk from his secretary confirmed her suspicion that Gunther did this all the time. She wasn't special, but simply another pathetic female writer who was willing to put out for a reading, a chance to find out if her script was the one.

Was I good enough for Gunther? Did I capture the magic he was looking for...the mystical quality needed to make it to the silver screen? Anger replaced the nausea, causing Grace to work her tense, stiff muscles mercilessly until she pulled a hamstring. Pain shot through her and she collapsed.

Dorrie raced over. "I told you not to dance."

"Thanks a bunch," Grace choked out, clutching her injured limb.

"I'm sorry. Come over here. Let's get some ice on that." She helped Grace up while the class took a five-minute break. Dorrie retrieved an ice bag from the small fridge in the corner of the room and placed it on Grace's leg.

"You're tight as a drum. What's going on?" The quizzical stare from her friend made Grace look away. No way was she spilling the truth. *Bad enough you did it. Now shut up about it.*

"Nothing."

Dorrie placed her hands on her hips and shifted her weight. "Don't lie to me, Grace Brewster."

"Let it alone, Dorrie. Let it alone." Tears gathered in the corners of her eyes. *Shit! I'm not gonna cry. No tears. None.*

The minute Dorrie saw the misting, her tone softened. "I'm sorry, Grace. What can I do?" She crouched down to be eye-to-eye with Grace, who was sitting on the floor.

"Nothing. I told you. Let it be, Dorrie." Grace grimaced as she pushed up to a standing position and limped out of the room. Once in her car, she blasted the radio, opened the windows, and raced down the highway to the home she shared with her sister on Benedict Canyon Drive.

Once inside, she poured a screwdriver, grabbed a bottle of ibuprofen plus a handful of ice, threw that in a paper towel, and hobbled out to the deck that surrounded the swimming pool. She lowered herself into a chair and placed the cold pack on her aching muscle. She washed down two pills with her drink and sat back. The sun warmed her chest and the tightness coiled inside her began to loosen.

Within fifteen minutes, the pain in her leg had subsided and she had drained her glass. Feeling grubby after her encounter with Gunther, Grace took a shower. Under the hot spray, she relaxed even more. Emotion gathered in her and tears flowed. She propped her head up against the tile and sobbed.

* * * *

Day after day, Grace checked her email, not once, but twenty times. Still no message from Gunther Quill about her script. *How long does it take to read a ten-page treatment?* She bit her nails, did laundry, swam laps, and avoided her dance class while she waited. As more days passed with no word, tension grew. Grace exercised at home to relieve the pressure.

While hiding from the world soothed her and allowed her to dodge too many questions from friends and family she didn't want to answer, she knew she couldn't escape Dorrie's caring curiosity for long. Before a week was out, her friend called. "When are you coming back to class?"

"When my leg is healed," Grace lied.

"Really? How come I don't believe you?"

"I can't help that."

"We're friends. What could be so terrible that you can't tell me?"

There was silence. *That I prostituted myself to sell a script?* She chewed her lip.

"Whatever it is, please call me. Let's have dinner. I'm worried about you, Gracie."

Hell, I'm worried about me, too. No morals.

"I'll call. I promise." Grace hung up the phone. She padded over to her computer to check her inbox for the one-hundredth time that day. This time, it was there. A message from Gunther. She held her breath as she opened it.

> *Dear Ms. Brewster,*
> *Thank you for submitting your script to Regency Hill Productions. Unfortunately,*
> *it's not what we're looking for at the present time. We hope you will submit your next one to us, and we wish you well in your screenwriting career.*
> *Sincerely,*
> *Marsha Durward*
> *Assistant to Gunther Quill*

Grace screamed as fury welled up inside. Feelings of worthlessness washed through her. *He didn't even have the decency to reject me himself. Used his assistant. I'm a stupid fool. He just wanted to get laid.*

Checking her phone, she discovered a series of texts from her sister. *Cara! Need to hear your voice. But I can't tell you why. You'll be ashamed of me.* With a badly shaking hand, Grace dialed through a flood of emotion.

"Hi, Pook—" Cara stopped when she was met with uncontrollable crying. "Grace? Gracie, what's wrong? Talk to me."

Grace took a couple of deep, shuddering breaths to calm herself. She couldn't speak.

"Please, darling, what's wrong?" Cara asked.

Silence. Grace tried to catch her breath but couldn't.

"Gracie, listen. Listen! You get on a plane and get out here right away, Grace Brewster. Whatever it is, we'll fix it."

Finally, she found her voice. "You can't, you can't…" Gracie dissolved into tears again and hung up. When she could control her emotions, she yanked a small suitcase from the closet, threw in some clothes, and closed up the house. *Cara's right. I've got to get out of L.A. I need her.*

Grace sat down at her computer and purchased a one-way plane ticket to New York. She made a sandwich and packed it in her purse before calling a taxi. She munched on an apple while she sat by the front gate, texting.

> *Will be on the nine o'clock red-eye tonight. What's your address?*

Seconds later, she received a reply.

> *The Stanford, Seventy-Fourth and Central Park West. I'll send a car for you.*
> *Driver's name is Bobby. Send me your flight number. Miss you so. Can't wait to see you.*

Grace sent the information then waited patiently for the cab. *I can't think about…what I've done. Can't take it in now. Have to forget. Move on. How can I? I'll never be able to forget.* She put her head in her hands and cried again.

By the time Grace boarded the plane, she was exhausted. The emotional toll of Gunther Quill's cold, manipulative behavior had depleted her energy. Being on the go all day with her pulled hamstring, which had stiffened up and began to hurt again, also wore her out. She closed her eyes and woke up three hours later. After a drink and an attempt to read the book she brought, Grace gave up, resigned to staring out the window, hoping to snooze through the rest of the trip.

She went back to sleep, only to awake during landing. Kennedy airport didn't have the usual hustle and bustle, but maybe that was because it was five in the morning. Gracie yawned and looked around for Bobby. She spied a short, attractive man with dark hair holding up a sign with her name on it, and she approached him.

"Hi, I'm Bobby," he said, offering his hand as he took her carry-on bag.

"Grace." She met his with hers.

"Your sister told me to take very good care of you," he said. Tears once again gathered in her eyes. Bobby put his free arm around her shoulders. "Don't worry, sweetheart, Bobby's got the reins now. Everything's going to be all right. You can tell me all about it in the car."

They retrieved her luggage from the baggage claim area, and Bobby toted everything to his beautiful town car. He handed Grace his handkerchief before he shut her door.

"What happened? Your sister is worried sick."

"Nothing."

"Nothing? Really? Come on, you can do better than that." Bobby moved the vehicle through the maze of roads leading to the highway.

"It's private. I can't talk about it," she mumbled.

"Did ya kill someone?" He shot her a glance in the rearview mirror.

"No!" She chuckled. "Not that I wouldn't like to."

"Got someone you want to have rubbed out?"

Her eyes widened. "You can do that?"

"Nope, but I got your attention."

She burst out laughing. "Cara didn't tell me I'd get a comedy routine on the trip."

"She forgot that? Geez. I'll have to talk to her. Yeah, I always try out my new material on passengers. Captive audience," he snickered.

"You do?"

"Gosh, they make 'em gullible in California. No. I just drive. Sometimes I provide a little guidance...a little wisdom. Always a sympathetic ear. But the comedy is spontaneous."

"I didn't think I could laugh anymore." She relaxed against the cushions and looked out the window.

"Never lose your laugh. You look a lot like your sister."

"She's the pretty one. I'm the studious one."

"Oh? You calling me a liar? If so, I'll have to drive you right back to the airport."

Grace smiled. "I'm not calling you a liar, that's just the way it's always been."

"Don't typecast yourself, honey. You're a beautiful girl. Guys here are gonna flip when they meet you."

"Think so?"

"Hey, I know great women when I see them. Don't tell my wife." He eased them onto the Long Island Expressway.

"You're married? Damn! All the good ones are taken." She frowned in mock disappointment. Now it was Bobby's turn to chuckle.

Traffic thickened as they approached Manhattan. Bobby seemed philosophical about the crush of cars. Grace asked him questions and kept him talking about his work, wife, and now two children. She was happy to keep the spotlight off herself as they rode through New York traffic.

Bobby carried her suitcase inside where Rex, the doorman, picked it up. She hugged Bobby farewell. "Thank you for making the ride so easy."

"My pleasure. I'm sure I'll see you again soon." He tipped his hat.

"Welcome Miss Brewster," Rex said.

"Grace," she said, extending her hand. He took it.

"Your family is anxiously awaiting your arrival. It's a bit early for them, but Miss Cara said to buzz whenever you got here, no matter the time."

My family. God, that sounds good. A small smile crept over her face. Rex placed her valise in the elevator and pressed the button for the fifteenth floor. When the door opened, Grace moved to pick up the heavy valise, but a tall, handsome, dark-haired man wearing a navy blue terrycloth bathrobe was waiting there and got it first. He introduced himself.

"Grant Hollings. Your soon-to-be-brother-in-law." He shook her hand. "This way."

Before she even got to the doorway, Cara, wrapped in a pink terry robe, flew out of the apartment and down the hall, enveloping Grace in her arms for a big hug. She flinched a little when she was squeezed.

"Oh, sorry. I forgot about your shoulder."

"No problem." Cara stepped back and ran her fingers through her sister's hair, staring into her eyes with a worried expression. Grace lowered her gaze to avoid the question hanging between them.

"I'm okay," she mumbled.

"That's not how you sounded on the phone," Cara said.

"I was out of control. But I'm all right now."

"What happened?" Cara put her arm around her sister as they walked slowly back inside.

"I did something…terrible. And I've been punished for it. I don't want to talk about it, okay?" She hung her head.

"Okay. But you're still number one with me, Pookie." The sting of tears made Grace blink.

"Pookie? Mom, you call your sister Pookie?" Sarah, Cara and Grant's daughter, bounded out of her bedroom to greet her new aunt. Wearing a frilly pink nightgown, her hair flying every which way, the young still girl resembled both older women.

"Only I'm allowed to call her Pookie, Sarah. Meet Grace."

"Aunt Grace. Can I call you Aunt Pookie?"

Grace laughed. Sarah flew into her embrace, and Grace no longer had time to be sad. The Hollings household burst into activity. Jane, Grant's sister dragged herself out of bed. She was now bunking in with Sarah so that Grace had a place to sleep.

"Who wants French toast?" she called out.

Everyone chimed in. Jane introduced herself to Grace then lumbered into the kitchen. Sarah skipped to the breakfront to retrieve placemats and napkins. Grant brought down the good dishes from the tall cabinet in the kitchen after placing Grace's suitcase in her new quarters.

Cara put her arm around her sister. "Like old times, when we were kids…" She teared up.

"Yup. Sunday nights with mom." Grace's eyes watered.

"What was that like, Mom?" Sarah asked as she arranged china and silverware on the dining room table. Cara sat down and pulled Sarah into her lap, wrapping the little girl in her arms. "Our mom would make a special dinner on Sunday nights. She'd pull out a jigsaw puzzle and pop a movie in the VCR. We'd eat, watch a romantic movie, and do our puzzle."

"Lots of laughing and good food," Gracie chimed in.

"Can we do that, too, Mom?"

"Sounds like a good idea. No performance on Sunday nights."

Grant entered the living room with two mugs. "For the Brewster sisters." He handed one to each.

"Does this have…" Gracie began.

"Light with one sugar, right?" She nodded. "Damn. Sure know how to make a girl feel welcome." She smiled at Grant, who returned her grin.

She took a sip of her coffee and sat down at the table. For a while, she forgot all about Gunther Quill and her rejected screenplay.

The phone rang and Cara answered it. "I have your copy of our script changes," she said then paused. "Come on over."

Chapter Two

"Gracie would you mind giving this script to Jake Matthews? He's going to pick it up in an hour. I need to go back to bed." Cara dropped the large envelope on the dining room table.

"No problem."

"Matinée Day. I've got until twelve thirty to get to the theater."

"Go, lady," Gracie said, giving her sister a playful shove. "I know you want alone time with Grant."

Cara blushed. "Where did you get that idea?"

"Know you too well," Gracie chuckled.

After being up so early, everyone else went back to bed, too, since it was Saturday. Pacing the apartment like a caged animal, trying to keep quiet, didn't calm her down. So Gracie covered her hair with a scarf and decided to clean. Cleaning relaxed her, always took her mind off her troubles.

Wearing rubber gloves, she was on her hands and knees scrubbing the kitchen floor when Rex buzzed from the lobby. It took Gracie a few minutes to figure out how to work the intercom, but she finally got it and gave the okay for Jake Matthews, Cara's Broadway co-star, to come up.

When she opened the door, there stood an incredible looking young man. He was about six feet two with perfectly trimmed, light brown hair on the short side, light brown eyes, shoulders as wide as a city block, and a smile that dazzled like sunlight. Her mouth hung open.

"Jake Matthews. I'm here to pick up an envelope?"

Gracie couldn't move.

"Are you the maid? Is Ms. Brewster here?" Jake peered past her down the hall.

"What?" She spat out. *The maid!* Grace smoothed out the apron she wore and removed the rubber gloves.

"Housekeeper perhaps?"

"I beg your pardon! I'm Cara's sister, Grace." She raised herself up to her full five foot four inches, straightening her back.

"Her sister? Half-sister? Different fathers? Her only sister?" He asked, adding insult to injury.

"Same father. Only sister. Wait here!" Grace controlled the urge to slam the door in his face. *He's Cara's co-star. Be nice. Be nice. Be nice.* She gritted her teeth as she walked down the hallway to the dining room to retrieve the envelope Cara had left on the table. Upon returning to the front entrance, she thrust it into his hand and started to shut the door.

He stopped it with his hand. "Cara has arranged for you to be my date for the premiere of my new movie next week." Frown lines on his forehead showed his hesitancy. "But if you'd rather not go, well, I understand. I mean you don't know me, and…you don't have to, I mean, I can go stag. It's just a premiere, no biggie or anything."

Her eyes narrowed as she watched him squirm. *So you think I'm too ugly to be your date, huh? You sleezeball.* Suddenly, her face changed. The angry, hostile look she'd been wearing melted away, replaced by a falsely sweet smile.

"Why I'd be thrilled to accompany you to your premiere. What a wonderful opportunity to get to know you better. And all those other movie stars. How delightful!" She gushed, fluttering her lashes and watching beads of sweat break out on his forehead.

"Well, then…I guess that's settled," he muttered.

She smiled. "When?"

"Next Saturday night. Around…let's see, movie starts at eight, so I'll be here at seven thirty."

"Perfect. I'll be ready. Formal attire?" She grinned at him and clasped her hands together.

"I guess. This is my first time." Perspiration from his chest soaked through his T-shirt a little bit.

Grace noticed it and grinned. *You haven't begun to squirm, Mister.* "Think it's formal. But you can ask Cara when you see her."

"Quinn'll know. Well…see ya," he said, backing away before he turned and almost ran down the hall.

Grace leaned her back against the door, dissolving into laughter. Cara wandered into the hallway, yawning. "Who was that?" she asked, stretching her arms straight up in the air.

"Jake Matthews."

"Did he get those changes?"

"He did. Told me you'd fixed us up for his premiere." She rested against the wall, giving her sister a penetrating stare.

"Oh, yes. Nearly forgot. You'll love him. He's perfect for you."

"Perfectly obnoxious and full of himself," Grace mumbled to herself.

"Any more coffee?" Cara stumbled into the kitchen.

He's going to get the surprise of his life! "Cara! Do you still have that dark pink dress?" Grace followed her. "I want to borrow it." Grace licked her lips.

"For your date with Jake?"

"Yep. It's perfect. I'll make him eat those words."

"What words?"

"Never mind. I've had enough of men who think they can push me around…God's gift to women. Time for a little revenge."

Cara turned to face Grace. "You're not going to do anything drastic, are you? I've got to work with him."

"Relax. I'll be my most charming self." *Just make him eat his words. I'll look so good, he won't even know it's the same woman. I'll have him begging for a goodnight kiss.*

* * * *

On Saturday night, Jane and Sarah were helping Grace dress for her date. An understudy was performing for Jake so he could attend, and Cara had to be at the theater. Pre-prep for what Gracie had dubbed "Jake's Earth-shattering date" had begun on Friday morning when Cara had joined Gracie for a facial, then on to the nail salon and the hairdresser.

The women had giggled like schoolgirls as they shared stories, old and new, while their nails were painted and their hair styled. Grace had missed being with Cara and had not seen her sister so relaxed and happy in years. She silently thanked Grant for Cara's calm demeanor and the improvement in her outlook. Sarah was a totally unexpected delight for Gracie, who was relieved to no longer be the youngest family member.

In town to close a deal for a client, Skip, Cara's agent, had stopped by for dinner. Since the show was doing well, he was no longer needed in New York and had returned to Hollywood. Skip and Jane had become friends. Grant had accepted him as well.

Gracie marveled at the constant bustle of activity in the Hollings apartment. Adults and children seemed to be coming and going all the time. Meals were often huge affairs, frequently including last minute guests. The mad dash of this new, warm family life soothed Grace's frayed nerves, and she regained her ability to smile.

Because it was December, Grace had decided to have some holly leaves woven into her hair. The sides were upswept, and it flowed in a gentle curl down her back. The dress was form fitting to the knee, but not too tight to sit down in, then it flared out. There were thin straps, and the front was cut low. The fabric was dark pink taffeta, so the dress shimmered and rustled when she walked.

Tall, silver satin sandals, a white wool cape, and long, silver gloves topped off the outfit.

"You look like Cinderella," Sarah said.

"Don't bend over. Even if you drop a hundred bucks," Jane warned with a snicker.

"I know."

"Why not, Aunt Jane? If she drops a hundred bucks?"

"Well, Sarah…"

"She means my bosom might come right out of my dress," Grace confided.

Sarah gasped, her eyes wide in horror. "Oh, no! That would be terrible! Embarrassing!"

"Right. So I'm going to stand up straight."

"Can you glue the dress on you?" the little girl asked. The two women burst out laughing.

"I almost wish I could." Gracie ruffled Sarah's locks. Just as Grace checked her gold watch, inherited from her mom, the buzzer sounded. Jane instructed Rex to let Jake up.

"I can't wait to see this. Can I let him in?" her eyes lit up.

"Sure."

The knock came not one minute later. Jane scurried down the hall to admit Jake. Sarah took a seat at the dining room table. Jake walked down the hall, and when he saw Grace, he stopped. A sharp intake of breath made her turn around.

"I don't believe we've met," he said, obviously dazzled.

"What? I'm Grace!" She rested her hands on her hips.

"No, really? I didn't recognize you. Last Saturday you were..." he began to cough and choke. Jane ran to get him a glass of water.

Didn't recognize me? Serves you right! Arrogant asshole. He took a sip and recovered. "You look amazing. You're beautiful. Really beautiful. Never would have known it from before."

"Do you always say whatever comes into your head, without filtering it through your brain?" She picked up her wrap.

He blushed. "Sorry. That wasn't very nice. I'm sorry."

Sorry? Not as sorry as you're going to be. He held her stole for her.

"I'll put it on in the lobby," she said, waving him off. He tucked it under his arm.

Grant moseyed out. "Don't keep her out late. Do you have a driver?"

"Cara lent us Bobby for tonight," Jake replied.

Grace smiled. "How wonderful, I love him!"

"Have a good time." Grant leaned over to peck Grace on the cheek. Sarah gave her a hug, and Jane simply waved.

As they walked down the hall, Jake blushed. "I was going to get you flowers, but I didn't think..." His voice trailed off.

Tears pricked her eyes. *He thought I'd be too ugly for flowers?* She was wounded, as if he had shot an arrow through her. The pain was short-lived, but intense. She couldn't speak and turned away from him to hide the hurt.

He put his hand on her bare shoulder. His touch made her tingle. "Hey. What's going on?" He bent down and peered at her.

"Nothing," she whispered.

"I meant I didn't think I could get you a corsage and be on time... What did you think I meant?"

"Oh." She sighed, dropping her gaze to her hands.

He stopped and closed his fingers around her upper arm. Pulling on her, he forced Grace to face him. "What's going on?"

He looked at her, but she averted her gaze so he couldn't see the truth.

"Nothing. I thought…I thought you meant something else. I was mistaken. Let's go."

"You didn't think I didn't buy flowers because I thought you were…unattractive…did you?"

"Do you…I mean, did you? You did. Of course you did. Never mind. Let's go."

"I want to straighten this out now…"

Her temper flared, and she raised angry eyes to his. "You do, do you? Don't tell me you didn't think I was ugly and didn't try to get out of this date. Because you did exactly that…because I was cleaning the house, you thought I was the maid. Then you simply decided I couldn't be Cara's sister because I wasn't pretty like her. Don't deny it. I saw it all over your face."

Jake stood silent, stunned. He colored.

"That's right, blush. You should. You should be damned embarrassed to treat any woman the way you treated me, and you didn't even know me. Shame on you."

He hung his head. "Would you rather cancel tonight?"

"Not on your life. I'm going to rub your nose in just how attractive I can be."

"You already have…have proven me wrong. I realize now it's never a good idea to judge so…quickly."

"Good. Let's go. I didn't get all dressed up to stay at home. You promised me a movie premiere, stars, a party…time to deliver."

He put his hand on her shoulder to stop her. She turned to him, trying to ignore the zing created by his fingertips on her skin. "I'm sorry if I offended you. I shouldn't have behaved that way. It's just that I was expecting…"

"You were expecting a Cara clone. And there was this grubby person, and you couldn't see beneath the dust and dirt to the woman underneath. I get it. I'm not dense, and I'm not stupid. But the way you behaved…like I was one of the ugly stepsisters, and Cara was Cinderella. Like I was the last person you'd want to spend an evening with…well, it pissed me off." As she recounted the encounter, the sting of tears pressed against the back of her eyes.

What the hell is the matter with me? He's nobody to me. What do I care what he thinks of me? If he thinks I'm pretty or not, so what? Gracie, where's your moxie? Don't let Gunther Quill rob you of your backbone, girl.

"What can I do to make it up to you?"

"Take me to the premiere and don't talk about it anymore." She turned toward the elevator with Jake following behind. They rode down in silence.

"You are going to talk to me tonight, aren't you?" She saw a bit of a hurt look on his face.

"Of course. I'm not an idiot or a game player who freezes you out in public."

"I don't know you at all, don't know what to expect."

"I guess you'll find out. There's Bobby." She waved at him.

"Looking mighty fine tonight, Miss Gracie."

"Thank you, Rex," she beamed at him.

Bobby got out of the car and opened the door for her. She stopped to give him a hug, and he laughed. "You're not supposed to hug the chauffeur," he whispered. "You're supposed to hug your date."

"I'll hug whoever I want," she chuckled.

Grace slid over, making room for Jake. He moved his fingers over, resting them on top of hers, but she slipped hers away and looked out the window.

"The silent treatment?"

She peered at his sad expression from under her blackened lashes. *Still incredibly handsome, even when he's pouting. And in that tuxedo. Wow.*

"Tell me about the movie. What's the story?" She turned to face him.

When they arrived at the theater, it was obvious she needed help getting up in the snug dress. Jake offered her his hand then raised hers to his lips for a quick kiss before they hit the red carpet. There was a loud cheer from a group of teenagers on the sidelines behind ropes.

Gracie smiled and stepped to the side so she wouldn't block him from his fans. Jake waved at the girls and then laced his fingers with hers. When they were inside, he stopped to mop the sweat off his forehead.

"You're afraid of those teenyboppers?"

"The movie. My first major role. Damn, I hope it's good."

I almost feel sorry for him.

"I'm sure you're fine." She refused to let him get under her skin. *Don't start falling for this creep.*

"Thanks a lot. Very comforting. It's no wonder you don't have a job as a nurse."

Her mouth hung open. "He's alive. He can shoot back. How do you know I'm not a nurse?" She narrowed her eyes.

"Your sister told me. Said you were a talented screenwriter. She said you'd done a great film. Can I read it sometime?" The reference to her script made her chest hurt.

"No. It's crap." Before he could respond, the ushers were showing them to their seats and offering to get popcorn and soda for them.

"I'm too nervous to eat, but if you'd like some?" Jake asked. She shook her head. "Can I hold your hand?"

"Like in the doctor's office?"

"Never mind. I shouldn't have asked. Sorry," he mumbled.

Lighten up, Gracie. She put her hand on top of his and gave him a little smile. He wrapped his fingers around hers and rested them on his thigh. She snuggled down into a comfortable position. It wasn't long before the lights dimmed and the movie came on.

* * * *

Damn! That was bad. Jake was awful! Crap, how am I going to pretend? She glanced over at him, and he wasn't smiling.

"Well done. Good job," she said, patting his arm, trying to appear sincere.

"I was terrible." He cast his gaze to his lap.

"I wouldn't say that…" She softened her tone.

"Oh, wouldn't you? Why not? Your perfect chance to gloat," he shot back.

Grace bit her lip to hold back the snotty reply itching to escape. As he stood up, she tried to paste a wan grin on her face. "Let's get out of here before the producers have my hide." Grace pushed to her feet.

"Too late," Jake muttered under his breath as three men in perfectly cut business suits strode up the aisle. They stopped to shake his hand. Murmurs of "nice job" and "great" greeted her ears. He didn't introduce her, and she was glad.

As they moved on, she spied a familiar figure coming their way and her heart stopped. *Gunther Quill!* He nodded to Jake, mumbling something Grace didn't hear because her ears weren't working. Everything in her body had ceased to move except for her heart, which was beating twice as fast as before. Gunther glanced to Jake's right and spotted her.

She felt color rush to her cheeks as he stared briefly at her with glittering eyes and a sly smile on his lips. Mesmerized at first, Grace eventually broke the spell and turned away. When she found the courage to look again, Gunther was gone. She breathed a sigh of relief.

"Hey, I'm sorry, that was Gunther Quill. I should have introduced you. You could give him your script."

"No, really...it's okay. Tonight is about you." *Let's get out of here before he comes back.*

"Come on. There's a private party in Westchester."

Bobby was there to pick them up, and before they could blink, he had maneuvered the car onto the West Side Highway, heading north. Grace's mind was reeling. *So that awful picture was Gunther's. Huh. Thought he was so smart.*

"The producers didn't think it was so bad."

"You were fine, really," she said, her mind elsewhere.

"Thanks. Damning with faint praise..."

"You don't want me to gush, do you? That's really not me."

"I gathered," he said, dryly. "The producers seemed to like it. They said I was good. I guess as long as they like me, I'll get more work."

"That's right. As long as the producers like it," she repeated, thankful not to have to invent any more lies. Sympathy crept into her heart, and she inched closer to him. A bump in the road jostled them so that their fingers came in contact. He looked over at her and moved his hand to cover hers.

"You are even more beautiful in the light from the street lamps."

"That's me. Dim lighting's always best."

"Don't put yourself down. That was a compliment."

His words sobered her. Her heart hurt. After being used and discarded by Gunther, her ego was in pieces. She considered herself to be the lowest type of woman, to do what she did. Trying to rid the images of their tryst on his sofa from her brain hadn't worked. *I deserve to be put down, way down.*

He drew her to him. Gazing up at his eyes that had been staring at her mouth, she knew he'd try to kiss her soon. Her hand on his shoulder felt his muscles work as he eased himself into her space. His touch on her waist almost burned her skin. *No, no, no! I'm not attracted to this idiot. Back off.* She glanced at his lips, noting how perfect they were.

She tried pushing away, but his chest was like a wall of iron. His mouth descended on hers and sparks flew. Panic set in, and she shoved harder. Obviously, he picked up on her signal because he backed off.

"Sorry. Never was good at reading girls. I thought you wanted me to kiss you. Wrong, again." He sat back on his side of the car.

She blew out a breath and retreated to her corner. *You weren't wrong, I was stupid.* They remained still, the only sound the hum of the tires on the road, until arriving at their destination. Bobby opened the door, letting in cold air. Grace shivered, drawing her cape closer around her .

"We'll probably be here for two hours, Bobby," Jake said.

"Brought my ereader. No worries."

The house was huge. The ultra-modern design had several stories of glass and weathered wood. The front lawn was terraced into three levels leading up to a large black door. Grace looked around with appreciation. *Wish our gardener was this good.* The grounds were immaculate, including a perfect stone wall hugging the long, circular driveway. Floor-to-ceiling glass windows showed a crush of people inside. Strains of rock music met their ears.

"Wow! This is some place," Jake said, his eyes wide.

"You're new to all this, aren't you?"

"Pretty much. I come from a small town—Willow Falls? It's upstate."

"Don't know it."

"Didn't think so." He smiled.

"Stick close to me. I've been to these things before."

"Good. Clueless here."

Don't get excited. He's a bumpkin. Not for you. And he thought you were the maid!

They entered, and Grace led him to the bar. "Helps to be holding a drink when you're trying to talk to people," she advised.

A bartender was pouring Cosmopolitans. Jake picked up two and handed one to Grace. She took a sip. *Wow, this is strong!* Jake took a hefty sip and smiled. An attractive woman about thirty-five years old, wearing a low-cut dress tight enough to be a second skin, sauntered over. Grace noticed her give Jake the once-over.

"You're the second guy in the movie, aren't you? Jason, I think his name was?"

Jake nodded. "And this is..." He gestured toward Grace, but the woman simply raised an eyebrow and turned her back. She linked her arm through his. Jake threw Grace an apologetic glance as she followed along behind them. The woman chattered away while Jake nodded in reply. Grace could hardly keep from laughing. *She's coming on to him, and he doesn't even know.*

Another rail-thin woman with short blonde hair joined them. "Mitzi's going to research costumes at the Met for that period piece Gunther's doing."

"The Met?" Jake asked.

"Not the Metropolitan Opera, darling. The Metropolitan Museum. Of Art. You know."

"Oh, oh, of course!" Jake put on a good performance, but Grace wasn't fooled. She could tell right away that he had no idea what they were talking about. He excused himself to get another drink. Grace was still nursing the first one and watched him return to the sophisticated women and pretend to know what they were discussing. Grace looked around the room to see if she spied any of her acting or camera friends, but no one looked familiar.

She turned and almost ran into Gunther Quill holding hands with a stunning blonde wearing a sexy red dress and a big, diamond ring. She gulped, searching frantically for an escape, but Jake was still deep in conversation.

"Don't run, my little bunny," Gunther oozed, taking her elbow. "Let me introduce you."

The blonde narrowed her eyes and stared at Grace.

"This is my fiancée, Elsa Marquette. Elsa will be starring in my newest movie. Elsa, this is Grace Brewster…Cara Brewster's little sister."

Fiancée! Elsa extended her hand and left Grace no choice. She couldn't breathe as her eyes sought the engagement rock Elsa was wearing. Sweat broke out on Grace's upper lip.

Elsa shot a phony smile at her before she spoke. "Gunther loves brunettes," she said. "Let's see…screenwriter or bit player?"

"Screenwriter," Grace mumbled, her eyes wide.

"Ah, of course," Else nodded. "You know what they say…gentlemen prefer blondes." Her eyes were so cold they'd freeze hell.

"Nice to meet you," Grace muttered, trying to remember what she'd been taught growing up. *She knows. She knows he slept with me!* Gunther stood staring at her. Lust glittered in his eyes. *He's laughing at me. Engaged! Oh my God. What have I done?*

Emotion caught in her chest. Bile rose in her throat and tears stung the backs of her eyes. *Fool, stupid fool. Of course he's engaged. I should be surprised he isn't married. Run!* She gulped down the rest of her Cosmo.

"Excuse me," she said, pointing to her empty glass as she moved toward the bar.

"Of course." Gunther bowed slightly, grinning as she slipped away to refill her glass and find a corner to hide in. She was sick to her stomach. Leaning against the wall, she took a healthy swig. The alcohol loosened her control and angry tears spilled over onto her cheeks.

"You okay?" The deep voice at her ear was Jake's.

"Nice of you to stay with your date. I see you have other women on your mind." She brushed her fingers across her face.

"You weren't exactly into me in the car. I figured you'd like it better if I left you alone."

"Whatever," she waved her hand, gazing at the drink in her hand.

"You're upset. What happened?" Jake tipped her chin up before he downed the rest of his Cosmo.

"Nothing." She avoided his gaze.

"I need another drink."

"I think you need some food. Where is it?"

He shrugged his shoulders. Grace hesitated to explore the house for fear of running into Gunther, or worse, Elsa, again. But Jake was getting plastered, and she needed to get something into his stomach. "There, there," Jake said, pointing.

Grace took his hand and pulled him to the *hors d'oeuvres table*. She picked up a plate.

"What do you like?" He mumbled something unintelligible. His glazed look told her the alcohol was taking effect. "Some of everything then." She picked up a pair of tongs and piled up cheese puffs, cold jumbo shrimp, stuffed mushrooms, mini quiche, and *crudités* on the plate.

Then she had to find a place to sit. "Come over here." She grabbed his lapel and pulled him over to a table. He took a healthy swig of his drink. "These are amazing," he said, licking his lips.

Her gazed rested on his tongue for a moment. *Stop looking at him like that.* Gracie shoved a cheese puff in his mouth.

He chewed quickly and swallowed. "What was that?"

"Cheese puff. Like it?"

"Yeah but not as much as the Cosmos," he wandered toward the bar with Gracie right behind. She stuffed a baby carrot in her mouth while Jake got a refill.

"You shouldn't have another one of those." She reached for the glass.

Jake snatched his drink away from her grasp and raised it high above her head. "I'm a grown man. I'll drink what I want. Why do you care, anyway? You don't even like me."

"I didn't say that."

"Didn't have to." He took a sip.

"Here, eat something."

He scowled at her. "Are you my mother?"

"The food is good."

"Then why don't you eat it?" he challenged her.

Her stomach was in a knot. Seeing Gunther made her appetite go south. She was barely able to choke down that raw veggie. *I can't tell him.* "I'm not hungry."

"That makes two of us."

Grace put the plate down on the table and sank into a chair that backed up to a wall. The loud music, the crowd…everything grated on her nerves. She'd been humiliated again by this man and his fiancée, too. Gathering what little dignity she had left, she pushed to her feet. "I'm leaving."

Jake raised his eyebrows. "The night is young." He made a sweeping gesture, almost knocking a drink out of the grasp of one of the women who had been talking to him before.

"I think you should, too," she said, taking his arm.

"Now you want me, eh?" He snickered then chugged the rest of his Cosmo. "Guess we're leaving."

When the cold air hit Grace in the face, the effect of the alcohol she'd consumed wore off. But not for Jake. He stumbled along, hanging on to her to keep from falling. They found Bobby's limo. He opened the door, and Jake fell in with Grace sliding in behind him.

"Why did you come with me if you hate me so much?"

"I don't hate you…I…just…you were pretty harsh, nasty…"

"Oh. When I first met you. Yeah. I was kinda dumb, wasn't I? I'm sorry. No hard feelings."

Bobby put the car in gear and pulled out of the driveway.

"Let's kiss and make up." Jake pulled her to him roughly and planted his lips on hers. Grace froze, letting Jake explore her mouth. *Even drunk, he can kiss.* In a minute, she regained her senses and pushed away, hugging the other side of the car.

"See. There you go. Not liking me again." He slapped his leg.

"I let you kiss me. What more do you want?"

He laughed. "You're kidding, right? You…in that dress? And you ask me what more do I want? I want it all, baby. I want you."

Grace noticed Bobby glancing at them in the rearview mirror. She was comforted by his presence. *Thank God he sees what's going on.*

"Don't worry. I'm not going to attack you. Hell, I've wanted plenty of women I couldn't have. No biggie."

She let out a breath and relaxed back against the seat. "Best news I've had all night."

"Ouch! You sure know how to hurt a guy."

"And you're still attracted to me?"

"Baby, you've no idea." They sat in silence, both staring out their own windows for fifteen minutes, until Grace sensed the heat of his stare and turned to face him.

"You're lovely, really...lovely." His eyes looked like pools of melted caramel. His gaze traveled over her body, lingering on her chest. "Who wouldn't want to make love to you?" He whispered.

He inched closer to her on the seat. She was drawn to the warm look in his eyes. He reached out to cup her cheek with his hand. "You were upset. Something bad happened to you tonight. But you won't tell me. Why won't you tell me?"

The softness of his tone wreaked havoc with the thick wall she had built around herself. Gracie wanted nothing more than to get lost in the arms of a caring man and cry about what happened. She longed to confess her mistake and humiliation, to mourn the rejection of her script. But Jake had had too much to drink. And he had put her down before he saw her dressed up. Wounded her, perhaps unintentionally, but even an error in judgment still hurt.

She remembered how it stung when he treated her like the ugly duckling. Always second to her amazing sister, his put down was magnified by years of being only second best. And the attentions of a drunken man, to be forgotten the next day...or worse, *rued* the next day, only made her wary. She didn't believe he wanted her. He wanted a woman, and she was there.

Jake was right up against her, nibbling her neck. Grace took a deep breath, bracing her hands against his strong chest. "You're so beautiful." He raised his palm to her breast and closed his fingers around the soft flesh. "I bet these taste as good as they look." He lowered his head.

"Keep your hands to yourself." Grace pushed him away so hard he fell back against the door on the other side. Stunned, he could only stare at her.

"Grace? Are you all right?" Bobby asked, his concerned frown reflected in the rearview mirror.

"Fine. Thanks, Bobby. I'm fine."

The questioning look in Jake's eyes made her want to laugh. "Don't get turned down much, do you?"

Bobby eased the vehicle off the Westside Highway and onto 79th Street. When he pulled up in front of her building, Jake insisted on getting out and holding the door for her. By now, the ride home had worked on Jake's belly, filled only with alcohol. She saw his face pale.

"Excuse me," he said, rushing over to the hedges on the side of The Stanford and bending over. The sound of him retching made her stomach turn. Jake stood up and wiped his mouth with his handkerchief.

"I'm sorry, Grace."

"I'll bet. The perfect ending to a perfect date." She gave a little laugh then a courtesy. Spike, the night doorman, scowling at Jake, held the door open.

"Can I call you?"

"Why don't you save yourself the trouble?" Gracie hurried into the elevator as the tears she'd been holding back broke through her defenses. When she arrived at the apartment, she went in quietly and headed straight to her room.

"Just a minute, Pookie," Cara appeared from the darkness. "How was the premiere, and your date with Jake?"

"Total bust," she said, shortly. "I'm tired. I don't want to talk about it."

"Was it that bad?" Cara's brow furrowed.

"I said I don't want to talk about it." Grace went into her room, and turned the lock. *She's not responsible.*

"Goodnight to you, too," Cara called in through the closed door.

Grace toed off her shoes, unzipped her dress, and threw herself down on the bed, sobbing. In a few minutes, she dragged herself up to finish undressing. Turning out the light, she slipped between the sheets and pulled up the down quilt against the chilly air. She couldn't get Gunther, Elsa, and Jake out of her mind.

Don't get mad, get even. As she waited for drowsiness to knock her out, a plan hatched. With a smile on her lips, Gracie drifted off to sleep.

Chapter Three

Before the sun was up, her dry mouth begged for water, waking Grace early with a huge thirst. The slight headache pounding at her temples told her she'd had a touch too much to drink at the party. *At least I wasn't wasted, like Jake.* She padded into the kitchen for a tall glass of water then put up a pot of coffee. *Guess I'm awake.*

Opening her laptop on the kitchen table, she created a new blog under the name *Movie Maven*. After filling a mug and taking a few healthy sips, she sat back to think. A grim smile crossed her lips as she started typing. *Payback time, Mr. Quill.*

> *Just in Time should be retitled Don't Waste Your Time. The new Gunther Quill romantic comedy is neither romantic nor a comedy. More like a comedy of errors—errors in writing, acting, and storyline.*
>
> *Jake Matthews plays Donnie, a goofy guy in love with the large-chested model next door…where have we heard that before? Only everywhere! I nominate, Mr. Matthews for the most-wooden-performance-of-the-year award. I wanted to take his pulse to see if he was still alive. As a romantic lead he has the sex appeal of a slug. His performance put me to sleep.*
>
> *Rhonda Dowling's I.Q. must be smaller than her bra size. But she's not to blame. The script lacks humor, decent dialogue, and an original, believable plot…but who am I to be so picky?*
>
> *Shame on you, Mr. Quill. After producing the fabulous Joe Martin series with that wonderful*

actor and gorgeous hunk, Quinn Roberts, what possessed you to produce this cliché-ridden clunker? Just In Time *stinks more than a rotten egg in a henhouse in August. Hey, Mr. Quill, I hear they're looking for baristas at the Starbucks on Hollywood and Vine.*

Save your money, moviegoers, watching paint dry is more interesting than viewing Just In Time.

The Movie Maven

Gracie clicked *publish*. Then she went to *Facebook* and *Twitter*.

I just read the funniest movie review!

She posted those words plus a link to her Movie Maven blog everywhere she could think of. *I may be small potatoes, Gunther Quill, but I will keep a few people away from your movie.* After refilling her cup, she closed her computer and opened her *Nook*. She selected a new romance book and settled down on the couch.

A nagging discomfort about her trashing Jake preyed upon her mind until she remembered his line, "bet those taste as good as they look" and the way he pawed her. Surprisingly, taking aim at Gunther and Jake didn't make her feel better.

Gunther still had succeeded in humiliating her and Jake had made her feel ugly then cheap. She did have to acknowledge that Jake had tried to make up for it before he barfed in the bushes. She snickered at the memory of how embarrassed he was. Unexpected sympathy for his pathetic drunkenness entered her heart. *So what? No one will see that blog. It's new. No followers. So I've dissed him to about a dozen people. Big whoop.*

After reading for a bit, Grace fell asleep. Sarah woke her up at eleven o'clock, chattering away while Grace prepared a bowl of cereal for her niece. She joined her with Cheerios and opened her laptop. *Might as well see how few people came to read my hatchet job.* She opened up the blog and checked the stats. Five thousand hits in four hours. *Wow!* Then she scrolled down to see the comments. *Oh my God, two hundred and fifty!*

> *Thanks for the heads up. You saved me ten bucks.*

> *Funniest review ever!*

> *Love your review.*

Comment after comment applauded her scathing words. Occasionally, there would be a couple of people chastising her for such harshness, but mostly the comments were positive. She read them all. *Huh. Imagine that!*

She sat back a little dazed and surprised. When she clicked on the stats again, half an hour later, five thousand had become fifteen thousand. *Hot damn! It's going viral.*

Scrolling through the comments, she noticed one from Tiffany Cowles, giving her an email address with an offer.

> *Wish to publish this review in* Celebs R Us. *Will pay fifteen hundred dollars. Call this number to talk about writing a regular review column for us.*

Grace wrote down the phone number and the email. She dashed off a response accepting Tiffany's offer and sending her a copy. *Yes, Ms. Cowles, I'd love to do a weekly column. What's the pay?*

Grace hit "send" and sat back, feeling proud of herself. *Viral? Thousands? In* Celeb 'R Us *I'll reach millions. Hah! Take that Gunther Quill!*

* * * *

Down the street from The Stanford on a high floor in the Wellington Arms, Jake Matthews dragged himself out of bed. His mouth was as dry as cotton. He was as thirsty as if he'd been in the desert for months. His head ached and his stomach was growling, but the idea of food made him retch.

How much did I drink last night? He groaned and slipped on his bathrobe. Jake had crashed at Quinn and Susanna Roberts' apartment. He had been much too drunk to go home so Bobby had called Quinn, who gave the go-ahead to drop Jake there.

Jake cracked the door open then shuddered as the sound reverberated through his body. The brilliant winter sun pouring through the living room windows stabbed Jake in the eyes. He padded to the private guest bathroom to wash up.

When he finally emerged, Quinn and Susanna were sitting on the sofa, coffee mugs on the table in front of them. Susanna was reading the paper while Quinn surfed the Net on his laptop. When Quinn's gaze met Jake's, he knew something was up. Quinn looked as if someone had died.

"It's just a hangover, Quinn. I'll be all right by performance time."

"What happened last night?"

Jake went to the kitchen for coffee. *Need about a gallon of this.* He popped two Ibuprofens into his mouth then washed them down. "I don't remember everything."

"Bobby said you were bombed out of your skull."

He sat down slowly. "Maybe I had one too many."

"Maybe?"

"Okay, okay…I was a little…drunk."

"How'd it go with Grace?"

All of a sudden, memories of the fiasco date came flooding back. Jake put his head in his hands. "Oh my God."

"Doesn't sound good," Quinn said. Susanna put down the newspaper.

"Terrible. Horrible. I was a Neanderthal. What did I do?"

"I dunno, Jake, what did you do?" Quinn chuckled.

"This is no laughing matter. I screwed up big time. Do you have the number of a florist?

"Why?"

"I gotta send flowers, a dozen roses… no, maybe two dozen."

Susanna smiled. "Quinn has a florist on speed dial."

"Hey, I don't mess up that often," Quinn protested.

"Often enough," she said, glancing at the vase of fresh pink roses on the sideboard in the dining room before picking up the paper again.

Quinn wrote down the number for Jake, who called immediately. "That's right, The Stanford. Message? Hmm. How about 'I'm so sorry about last night. You deserved better.'?"

Quinn nodded.

"That's it, then. When'll they be delivered? Can't you get them over there today? I really need them there today. What? Okay, charge me the rush fee. Yeah."

"So what exactly did you do, Jake? If you don't mind me asking," Susanna said.

"Yeah. Spill it."

Jake outlined most of the evening, but stopped at the car ride home.

"Come on, Jake. That isn't a dozen roses evening. What else? Give!"

Jake took a deep breath and rubbed his stubbly face. "Yeah, well, there was one other thing..."

"Come on, Jake. I'm on pins and needles here." Susanna turned her attention away from the news to look directly at him.

"I kinda...sorta...attacked her?"

"You attacked her?" Quinn's eyes grew wide and Susanna gasped.

"Not really attacked. I got a little carried away and went right to...ah...second base."

"What did she do?"

"She shoved me against the car door."

"Good for her. What were you thinking?" Susanna straightened up.

"He was thinking what he'd like to do to her, right?" Quinn snickered.

"Guess so. I don't remember much. I said something, too. Something that really pissed her off."

"What?" They both asked together.

Jake could feel heat travel up to his face. He shook his head.

"You tell us, or I'm throwing you out on your ass, buddy," Quinn said, pushing to his feet.

Jake hid his face in his hands. "Bet they taste as good as they look," he muttered.

Quinn gave a low whistle while Susanna burst out laughing. "If you had said that to me, you'd be limping right now."

"You've got balls, Jake. Maybe you should've sent two dozen roses."

"I can't believe I said it either. It's like anything in my head just came right out of my mouth. Hey, I mighta thought that, but I've never said anything like it to a woman…not on the first date! Geez." He shuddered. "Oh, one other thing…"

"Yeah?"

"I barfed in her bushes."

Quinn and Susanna cracked up. Then Susanna stood up. "Come on, time for food. You need to put something in your stomach."

"I don't feel hungry."

"Force yourself. It'll make you feel better."

"I couldn't feel worse…"

"Yeah? You could be facing her instead of us."

Jake cringed. "Oh, God. I can't face her until those flowers arrive."

Susanna left them for the kitchen.

"So she was hot, eh?" Quinn glanced at Jake.

"Hot? Beyond smokin'. That dress…if it had been any lower, she would've been arrested. After what I said to her…thought she was the maid. Oh boy. I'm amazed she went out with me." Jake was greeted by silence. He looked up at Quinn, who was frowning. His eyes were darting along a page on his computer screen, his frown deepening. "Quinn?"

"Oh, buddy. Your day has just gone from bad to worse. A whole lot worse."

"What?" Jake leaned forward.

"*Just In Time should be retitled, Waste of Time…*" Quinn read.

* * * *

Grace played *Monopoly* with Sarah on the dining room table. Her laptop was open, and every half hour or so, she'd check it to see how the traffic on her Movie Maven blog was doing. The numbers leapt up by the thousands then the tens of thousands. After five hundred comments, she didn't even bother to read them. Once the hits topped one hundred thousand, she was giddy, almost lightheaded. *I never thought anyone would pay attention. Never expected anything like this.*

Cara joined them for a few moments before she left for the theater. "I hope your date last night wasn't too bad because I've invited Jake to come for Christmas Eve and Christmas Day with us. He'll be bunking on the sofa."

"What?" Gracie straightened up.

"We're doing a matinée on Christmas Eve and a performance on Christmas Day, so Jake can't make it home to his family."

"Do we have to have him here?" Grace chewed her lip. *Damn. Hoping I didn't have to face him.*

"He's my friend and colleague..." Before Cara could finish, the doorman buzzed. "Let him up, Rex." A minute later the doorbell rang. Cara brought in a dozen perfect red roses in a vase. She put them on the dining room table and tipped the delivery man.

"Roses!" Sarah squealed. "From a fan, Mommy?"

"They're for Aunt Gracie." Cara handed the card to Grace.

After reading the message, she muttered to herself, "Damn right."

"Uh oh. Aunt Gracie said a bad word," Sarah commented.

"I'm afraid Aunt Gracie does use bad words from time to time..." Cara said.

"Who's using bad words?" Grant piped up. Wearing jeans and a flannel shirt, he joined them in the dining room.

"Me. Bad training. Blame Carol Anne," Gracie said.

"That was mom's job to teach you not to use bad words." Cara moved over to give Grant a hug. He leaned down and kissed her.

"Guess she failed then," Gracie laughed. Cara reached over and snatched the card away from Grace and took off.

"Hey! Give that back." Grace chased Cara, who was one step ahead, reading the message while running around the house with her sister in hot pursuit. "It's personal!"

Cara stopped. Her expression became serious as she handed the note back to Gracie. "What happened last night?"

"Nothing."

"This isn't the place...but I want to know. Are you all right?"

"Perfectly." Grace picked up the vase and placed it on the coffee table.

"But it says—"

"I know." She cut her sister off. "And that's private. No explanations."

"Maybe I shouldn't have invited him…"

"It's fine! Cara, please! Butt out, okay!" Grace raised her voice, grabbed her laptop, and then sped to her room, slamming the door shut. She read it again. *Damn right I deserved better.* But she was mollified. *At least he apologized.*

Grace dressed with a little more care than usual for her trip to the theater with Cara. As Cara's secretary, she handled a wide variety of tasks, from helping Cara file taxes to emergency wardrobe pressing and makeup. They rode together in the limo, with Bobby at the wheel.

"Bobby, what happened last night," Cara asked, leaning forward, her hand on the partition between driver and passengers. Grace held her breath.

"I just drive, Cara. I can't watch in front and behind me, too."

Cara turned to her sister. "Come on, Pookie, give."

"Okay, okay. You're so pushy!"

"I worry about you."

"Yeah, I know. Too much. I'm twenty-seven, and can take care of myself."

"I don't know, Pook. This is a rough business. So…?"

"Jake got drunk and a little handy in the backseat."

Cara's eyebrows shot up. "Handy? Like fixing things?"

"You know, a little gropy. Touchy-feely. Do I have to spell it out for you?"

"Got it."

"I set him straight, and he stopped. Today, he apologized with flowers. Period. End of story."

"Is that everything?" The crease between her eyebrows deepened.

"Oh, wait. I forgot. He blew lunch in the hedges in front of our building," Grace chuckled.

Cara smiled. "Guess he was over-loaded…get it?"

"Still with the bad puns?" The women laughed as Bobby pulled up to the curb in front of the stage door. Cara slid out first. Grace stopped at the front window of the car. "Thanks for not telling, Bobby."

"No problem."

Grace rushed to catch up to her sister and barreled right into Jake. He caught her, gripping her upper arms. She looked up into his eyes and froze, feeling the warmth of his hands right down to her toes.

"Did you get the flowers?"

"They're beautiful. Thank you." His liquid gold eyes stared right into hers.

"Do you forgive me?"

"Of course."

He let out a breath. "Whew. Good. Not having a great day here and that would've made it a whole lot worse." He rubbed the back of his neck.

"Oh? What's wrong?" Grace bit her lip. *Please don't let it be my review.*

"Some bitch wrote a scathing review of *Just In Time*. Ripped me to pieces."

Grace's pulse kicked up. "Who is it?" *Please God, no.*

"Don't know, she signed it 'Movie Maven.' Coward. Afraid to sign her real name. I'd like to give her a..." he said, his hands fisting at his sides.

Grace took his arm and continued down the hall. "I understand you're coming to our house for Christmas?" She changed the subject before he could get graphic.

"Yeah. Too far to go back to Willow Falls."

"Is this your first Christmas away from home?"

He blushed. "How'd you know?"

"Lucky guess." *Unsophisticated, country bumpkin. Cute country bumpkin.*

"I have two sisters, one older and one younger. And a niece and nephew. Christmas won't be the same without them."

"Cara's the only family I have. Now, I've got a niece and a brother-in-law...well almost in-law."

"Cara's fiancé? Do you like him?"

"Grant's great. They're so cute together. They're what love is." She stopped at Cara's dressing room.

He leaned against the wall and looked down at her. "I hope you know how sorry I am. My...libido or whatever got the best of me. I don't usually get so...familiar or drunk on a first date. Hope you'll give me another chance." He rested his hand on her shoulder and again a tingle emanated from his touch.

"Oh?" She cocked an eyebrow. "You usually wait until the second date to get blasted?" She chuckled.

He laughed. "At least!" Grace opened the door. "See ya later. Break a leg."

He turned away and sauntered down the hall. Grace blew out a breath and watched him walk away. His jeans were just tight enough to outline his long legs and perfect butt. She noticed the slight pull of his flannel shirt, as it strained to cover shoulders so broad. They seemed even wider because his hips were so narrow.

Her gaze followed him for a bit, feeding the electricity running through her. *Maybe he's not so bad. Can't ever let him find out I'm Movie Maven. Never.* She entered Cara's room.

"There you are. Gabbing with Jake? Can you sew this seam for me?"

"What you do to a costume…" Grace shook her head slowly. "Outta be a law, lady. Give it to me. Where's the sewing kit?" Gracie closed the door and went to work.

Chapter Four

Gracie couldn't control her emotions on Christmas Eve, the first holiday where she and Cara had a family again. Gracie missed her mother, who had made a big occasion out of every holiday, trying to make up for the fact that their father had taken a powder. Trudy Brewster had worked hard, often juggling two jobs so her girls could have everything. Carol Anne and Gracie had taken dance lessons and singing lessons...even art classes after school.

Christmas was a major affair in their house, beginning on Christmas Eve. Trudy had had a ton of friends so they had hosted an open house, if she didn't have to work. The three of them cooked and baked for days, singing Christmas carols, arguing over who was off-key, and getting covered in flour. Times with Trudy were always happy times for Gracie. She adored her mother and sister. They took good care of her, doting on her as the baby.

By junior high school, each girl had a part-time job. Cara worked harder than Gracie because she was older. She waitressed on Friday and Saturday nights at the local diner and did babysitting during the week. Gracie was "the brain" of the family. So Trudy made sure child care jobs didn't interfere with her daughter's schoolwork.

When Cara had Sarah, Trudy moved in to help take care of her granddaughter. Their arrangement worked for the first year and a half, until Cara got sick and Trudy was killed in an auto accident. Grace still chokes up when she remembers the call. One day, she was confident and optimistic, fueled by her mother's loving support, the next, her mom was gone, and Gracie was destroyed.

Cara refused to let Gracie quit college to help with Sarah. So Cara did the only thing she could, she called Grant, Sarah's father, and gave him custody.

This Christmas they would have happier times, which had not been true of holidays since Trudy Brewster died. Sarah refused to allow Gracie to feel sad. The youngster boosted excitement about Christmas for the whole crew.

Sarah recruited Grace to help plan Christmas decorations, including a tree, go on secret shopping trips, and set aside time to bake together. Grace caught Christmas fever from her. The two became self-appointed, holiday elves around the Hollings household.

Grant's sister, Jane, had moved in with her boyfriend, Gary Lawrence. They were coming for Christmas day after spending Christmas Eve with Gary's family. There would be a full house, lots of noise and mouths to feed, presents to open, and gags to laugh over. Excitement was building in Gracie's heart as she made list after list of chores to be done, gifts to be bought and food to be cooked.

Since there was only a two o'clock matinée performance that day, in honor of Christmas Eve, festivities began at a normal time. Grace was planning to serve a fabulous dinner at six thirty.

"Jake's bringing his keyboard. We need a piano in this house." Cara turned around slowly, eyeing the living room.

"Where would you put one?" Grant asked, resting a hand on her shoulder.

"Don't know yet. But I'm working on it."

"Jake has a keyboard?"

"Yep. He's musical. His mom's a music teacher. He plays piano and sings rather well. I'd love to do a musical with him." The buzzer interrupted, and Sarah ran to talk to Rex on the intercom.

"It's Jake!" The little girl hollered.

Gracie scurried into her room to comb her hair and refresh her lipstick. *What am I running for? Primping for that country boy? Why? Not like we're going anywhere. Two different ways of life. Still, Cara says, "Always look your best."*

Sarah waited at the door and opened it for him. He was loaded down with Christmas gifts, an overnight bag, and his keyboard. Grace grabbed his keyboard before it hit the ground.

"Moving in?" she asked, a mischievous smile on her lips.

"Into your room, possibly?" he joked. Grace could feel the blush creep up her neck.

"Come on. You can put your bag in my room until tonight." She let him into her small room and Jake dumped his bag on her bed.

"Nice. I could be very comfortable in here."

He's only flirting. Grow up, Grace. Do you even care? Jake leaned down to touch her lips with his, but she pushed away. "My sister invited you here, I didn't." *Resist. Good looks, nothing more.*

"You're still mad at me?"

"No, but that doesn't mean I want contact, either." *Liar.*

"Come on, Grace. I'm stone cold sober. Don't you feel the chemistry between us? I only want a little Christmas kiss. Is that such a big deal?" She stood silently debating with herself. A look of exasperation swept over his face. "Never mind. Merry Christmas, Scrooge," he said in a sharp tone as he brushed by her.

He left the room, laden down with brightly wrapped packages. When he entered the living room, Sarah gave him a hug and Grant a manly handshake. Jake deposited his gifts under the huge, fragrant, beautifully decorated tree in the corner by the window. Grace hung back, leaning against the archway, watching.

"Something sure smells good." Jake avoided her stare.

"We have ham tonight, turkey tomorrow, lots of cookies...I made some of them...and a bunch of other stuff," Sarah said, bouncing from lap to lap.

"Have a drink," Grant offered. "Or would you like this hot, mulled wine instead of the usual?"

"Hot mulled wine? Haven't had that in a long time."

"Grace made it." Jake's gaze flickered over to hers for a moment before he turned his attention back to Grant, who scooped up a cupful for the young man. The sideboard in the dining room was set up with serving pieces. A tray with *crudités*, olives, and dip was on the coffee table. Jake relaxed on the sofa while Grace got busy in the kitchen.

"Quinn and Susanna are going to stop by tomorrow after the show. They're headed to Pine Grove and his sister's house tonight," Cara said. "Play for us, Jake."

He set up his keyboard while Grant found him a chair. "Which carol do you want to start with?"

Cara glanced between Jake and Grace, who hugged the doorway.

"How about 'Adeste Fidelis'?" He said, playing the first few bars. Grace paled. When she heard Cara's clear voice ring out, she ran into her room and slammed the door, which bounced back, remaining ajar.

Grace threw herself down on the bed, but picked up her head when she heard Jake's faint words coming from the other room.

"Gee, I didn't think my playing was that bad?"

"It's not you, it's that song. It was our mother's favorite. Be right back." Cara went into the hall and knocked softly. "Pookie, it's me. Can I come in?"

"Go away," Grace said through the small opening.

Cara gently pushed her way in. "Don't blame Jake, he didn't know. Come on, what's really bothering you?"

"Nothing. I'm fine. Just missing mom." Cara sank down next to her sister, so she could look into Grace's eyes.

"Pookie, you're not fine. You're troubled. Something has happened, or is happening, and I want to help you, but I have to know what it is."

"You can't help me, Cara. You can't. I'm stupid. I made a mistake. I'll get over it…eventually. Please, just leave it alone." Grace stared at her hands.

Cara sighed. "I suppose you're too old for me to force it out of you. I wish you'd open up. There's nothing so terrible you can't tell me. We can get through this together."

"Please, Cara. I know you mean well, but I have to deal with this on my own."

"Does it have to do with Jake? Poor guy. Out there mooning around, giving you longing looks, and you won't even glance at him. Is it because of what happened at the premiere?"

"It's complicated. He's not mooning. How many times do I have to say…I don't want to talk about it."

Cara pursed her lips, let out a breath, and then hugged Grace. "Whatever it is, I love you. You're my sister no matter what." The women stood up. Grace took a deep, shuddering breath.

"I know mom's songs make you miss her. I miss her, too. Don't you think she'd be so proud of Sarah?" Cara's eyes watered. Grace gave her a hug. "We have a house full of people who love us and want to celebrate. You and I have to dig down inside and find a place to be happy along with them," Cara said, wiping her eyes with her sleeve. "Think you can do that?"

Grace nodded. Together they returned to the living room.

"How about 'Jingle Bells'?" Jake asked, his gaze darting from sister to sister.

Gracie managed a small smile and a nod as Jake began to sing with the sounds from the keyboard. Sarah and Grant joined in. Then Cara and lastly, Grace, who stood directly behind Jake, resting her hand on his shoulder.

* * * *

Jake played a few songs until dinner was served. An amazing buffet of ham, scalloped potatoes, Jane's famous mac and cheese, Brussel sprouts, salad, homemade biscuits, and homemade applesauce with raisins crowded the sideboard and table.

She doesn't want me here. Why did I come? Stupid. Pushing yourself on her. Give her some space. Jake filled a plate with food and took a seat next to Sarah. He noticed Grace glance at him and frown. *If you want me to sit next to you, be nice to me.* He turned his attention to the young girl.

"Are you worried Santa won't find you here with us?" Sarah asked him as she took a forkful of mac and cheese.

Jake stifled a smile. "From what I hear, he can find you anywhere. So I'm not worried."

"Ewww. You're gonna eat those? Yuck!" Sarah pointed to Jake's Brussel sprouts.

"Sarah, don't make fun of someone's food choices," Grant said.

"I love Brussel sprouts, Sarah. You will too, when you get older. They're an acquired taste, adults only," Jake offered as he took a forkful of the vegetable.

"Ack-choired?"

"It means developed over time, not something you like right away," her father explained.

"Lotta big words." She turned her attention back to her food.

"That's the best mac and cheese I've ever eaten," Jake said.

"My aunt Jane makes it. Yeah. I think it's the best, too." Sarah beamed a slightly toothless smile at him.

"What's the going rate from the tooth fairy these days?"

"I got two dollars."

Jake whistled. "Wow! I only got fifty cents."

Sarah looked at him sideways. "That means you must be pretty old." Jake burst out laughing.

"Sarah!" Cara's eyes grew wide.

"Compared to Sarah, I am old. I'm more than four times as old as she is."

The little girl nodded. "That's old, Mommy."

Grace smiled broadly, and her eyes sparkled. Jake's gaze met hers over the table. *She has a beautiful smile.* Their eyes held for a moment before she looked away. *She's here then gone.*

"How did you get into this crazy business, Jake?" Grant asked.

Jake put down his fork. "I majored in theater at Kensington State."

"And then," Cara coaxed. Jake watched Grace pretend not to listen, but he spied her paying close attention.

"I got a shot for a walk-on at the Pine Grove Playhouse. The next season, I got a starring role and, lucky for me, there was a producer in the audience."

"Did Gunther discover you?" Cara asked.

Grace choked on a bit of ham, and Grant patted her back until she could take some water. *Why should his name make her choke?*

"As a matter of fact he did."

"Huh, don't think of Gunther Quill as hawking talent in regional theaters."

"So Quill discovered you and the rest is history?" Grant asked.

"Sort of. I'm from Willow Falls, a whistle-stop small town, where the University is. I'm still getting used to Hollywood and New York."

"You're great in the play. If I didn't trust Cara, I'd say she's more in love with you than me," Grant joked.

Jake blushed. "Thanks."

"Mommy! You don't love Jake more than Daddy, do you?" Sarah wailed.

"Daddy's kidding, pumpkin," Cara soothed her daughter and shot a sharp glance at Grant. "I love Daddy most of all."

Again, Jake's eyes met Grace's across the table. Her look was warm but how warm? *Is that a "let's be friends" smile or something more? Does she have feelings for me? What does she really think of me? Damn, she's the hardest woman to read...ever.*

The dinner was convivial, with everyone laughing, joking, and practically inhaling the excellent food. After the main course, they took a break to sing more carols. A smile swept across Jake's face when Grace came up behind him and rested her hand on him again. Her tender gesture sent flames through his veins. *Will I ever be able to touch her again? Even just to put my arm around her? Or will she always be leery because I was a jerk?*

The sound of her melodious voice in his ear was exciting because it meant she was standing close to him. He leaned back a little until he made contact with her, igniting sparks in him. She didn't move away. *Maybe her ban on connecting has been lifted?*

Cara read *'Twas the Night Before Christmas,* giving it her best performance. Sarah was mesmerized. Afterwards, Grant slung her over his shoulder like a sack of potatoes and carted her off to bed amid her howls of protest. One by one, the adults filed in to say goodnight when the young girl was tucked in.

Grant offered everyone a liqueur or sherry, and the four remaining sat and chatted until the drinks were gone. Finally, Cara and Grant made their excuses and toddled off to their room. *It must be great to go to bed every night with someone you love so much.* An inadvertent sigh escaped his lips as he watched the couple disappear behind their bedroom door.

"Thinking about wedded bliss?" Grace interrupted, reading his thoughts.

Jake sensed color rise to his cheeks. "It must be nice...they love each other so much. I mean, going to bed every night with someone you..." he stopped, flushing deeper at the realization of what he had said.

"Yeah, I know. Just the cuddling alone might be worth the price of marriage."

"Price of marriage?" Jake cocked his head slightly.

"I mean...what you give up and all to be married." A blush crept into her face, making her even more beautiful to him.

"I always thought it meant you were getting something, not giving something up."

"Different points of view, I guess."

Jake agreed and a silence fell between them. He looked at his watch. *Eleven. Time for bed. Tomorrow will be an early day.* He yawned and stood up.

"Oh! I'm standing in your bedroom, and you want to go to sleep. Sorry!" Gracie jumped to her feet and left abruptly, waving to him and calling "goodnight".

Jake sighed. *Not even a goodnight kiss.* He knocked on her door before calling in, "My bag?"

Gracie handed him his valise. "Sorry to disturb you," he said.

"No problem. Sleep well. Sarah will probably be up early. Best to catch some winks while you can." Jake nodded, took the bag from her, and headed for the bathroom.

* * * *

Gracie had never seen her sister truly in love before. The obvious joy that Grant and Cara shared in being together after so many years apart was infectious. They were never far from each other. They seemed always to be touching, arms draped over each other, holding hands, or even just entwining pinkies at the dinner table.

The scene touched her heart and cheered her spirit. *Cara deserves to be happy. Maybe I'll be that lucky someday and find someone like Grant who can love and forgive.*

In bed, trying to sleep, Gracie's mind kept moving though her body lay still. She glanced at the clock. *Three o'clock.* She pulled down the covers and pushed to her feet. Winding her ivory fleece robe around her naked body, she crept silently into the hall.

Though the room was lit only by moonlight, the outline of Jake on the sofa was unmistakable. An urge to crawl under the covers and cuddle with him gripped her. *You don't even know him!* The cool night air sent a shiver through her body as she padded soundlessly into the large room. Her gaze was drawn to the whiteness falling by the window. She stopped, leaning against the window sash and watched the light snow.

Hearing a noise behind her, she whirled around, her heart skipping a beat. Jake stood behind her, the blanket wrapped around his waist, his chest bare.

"I'm sorry, I didn't mean to disturb you," she whispered.

"You didn't. I wasn't asleep."

"No?" She swallowed. *Oh my God.* She was drawn to the tantalizing view of his torso.

He shook his head. "Too much on my mind, I guess."

"Me, too." She looked away, avoiding the probing stare from his light eyes. His bare chest disturbed her in the nicest way. *He should put something on.* Her pulse kicked up. He moved up next to her and turned his attention to the sight outside. "Snow."

"A white Christmas." Grace sang a line from the song softly.

He grinned. "I love a white Christmas. Must be snowing buckets upstate. Tomorrow the kids'll be sledding down McArthur hill," he sighed.

"You miss them, don't you?"

He nodded.

"The price of fame."

"Yeah. This business…"

She saw his eyes water a bit and placed her hand on his arm for a moment. Jake blinked a few times and smiled at her. As she turned to face him, she couldn't help but notice his chest, shadowed by the light from a street lamp. Covered in light brown hair, his pecs looked solid and his abs lean and defined. The muscles in his shoulders invited her touch to test their firmness.

Wonder what it would feel like to run my hand down him? Gracie tried not to stare, but knew he'd seen her wide-eyed expression as she studied his body. *For such a shy man, he doesn't seem to be shy about being half naked here with me.*

"You miss your mom, don't you?"

She tore her gaze from his body and rested it on his face as she gave a brief nod in answer to his question. "She tried so hard to make it up to us for being a one-parent family. She was like having two parents. Holidays were special times. We all stopped working to play together."

"You worked as a kid?"

"Yep. Mama's helper at thirteen. Babysitting when I was fourteen."

"Me, too. First delivering papers at eleven, then in my dad's auto shop."

"You know car repair?"

"Like the back of my hand. When I graduated high school, my dad wanted me to join him."

"Is he disappointed you didn't?"

"Not anymore. Since I've made a couple of movies. But he was at first. We didn't speak for a while."

Gracie touched his shoulder, ignoring the sizzle that leapt into her body at the contact with his skin. "How awful!"

"It wasn't good. But I had to go my own way."

"I'm glad you did. You're a good actor," she said.

"Not according to Movie Maven." He gave a short laugh. At the sound of her pen name, Grace stiffened. *Crap!*

"Don't worry. I'm not letting her get me down," he said, taking the opportunity to casually drape his arm around her. She didn't move out of his embrace.

"Maybe your role in *Blind Love* is a better role." Grace took a deep breath to calm her nerves. The fear he'd find out she was Movie Maven, plus his touch, kicked her pulse into high gear.

"I love the play. And doing it live every night is such a high. Applause is addicting."

She inched a little closer, lured by his fresh, masculine scent mixing with the aroma of pine. He picked up on her movement and eased her into his shoulder. A small sigh escaped her lips as they watched in easy silence while snow blanketed the city. She snaked her arm around his waist and snuggled into him.

Jake leaned over and kissed her hair. His intimate gesture broke the spell, causing Grace to pull away slightly, her eyes searching his. He lifted his arm to point to the ceiling.

"Mistletoe." He grinned. Gracie looked up and saw the little red-and-green plant hanging directly above them. While her chin was tilted up, Jake swooped down to brush his mouth gently against hers. When she didn't resist, he drew her up against him. Lowering his head a second time, he pressed his lips to hers and kept them there.

At his touch, a fire ignited inside Grace. She was helpless to resist and embraced him as he kissed her. When he stood upright again, his eyes glowed with passion. Grace tried to control her breathing. *No one has ever kissed me like that before.*

"Merry Christmas, Gracie," he whispered.

She stared at his mouth. Jake took the hint and kissed her again, but this time he swiped his tongue over her lips, and she opened. He angled his head to deepen the kiss, causing her to melt against him. With both hands occupied holding her fast, the blanket slipped to the floor, and Jake was left in only his boxers.

As his fingers dug lightly into her back, she slipped her palms up his chest, stopping at his neck. Their bodies fit together perfectly. Desire raced through her veins. Gracie wanted more. Jake's hand slipped down to her bottom and squeezed. Then he stepped back.

"You're not wearing anything?" Gracie saw his chest rise and fall in ragged breaths.

She shook her head. "I sleep nude."

Color rose up his neck as he backed away from her. "Not that I wouldn't like to...love to...but this is neither the time nor place..."

"I agree." She stated flatly, cutting him off. But her body was screaming at her to continue. Folding her arms across her breasts, she turned to face the window again and attempted to resume normal breathing while Jake stole up behind her.

"Did you feel it? The chemistry?" he muttered in her ear.

She couldn't deny it because the feeling was still racing through her veins. Slowly lifting her gaze to his, she smiled and nodded once. He stroked her hair then ran his finger down her cheek. "Beautiful Grace..." he uttered so softly she almost didn't hear. He pulled her into his embrace.

Grace rested her head on his chest, listening to the rapid, steady beat of his heart, and closed her eyes. *So this is what Cara feels when Grant holds her?* She sighed and relaxed against him. *It's wonderful.*

The Grandfather clock in the hall chimed four, startling the would-be lovers. They jumped apart then chuckled at their own skittishness.

"I suppose we should get some sleep," she said.

Jake yawned. "Before all hell breaks loose tomorrow."

"Right." Gracie tightened her sash and raised her gaze to his. "Good night."

"Good night."

She padded quietly back to her room, stopping at the door to watch him rearrange the blanket on the sofa. Their eyes met, she raised a hand, and then disappeared into her room.

Morning came before she was ready, the light shooting through curtains she forgot to draw woke her up. Sarah's shrieks about Santa having come woke the household. She dragged herself out of bed, slipped on a nightshirt, and strolled into the kitchen. Jake was measuring water into the coffeemaker when she entered. He hadn't even combed his hair and looked beyond adorable. *What man wakes up so cute?*

He stepped up behind her as she was opening the refrigerator door. Slipping his arm around her waist, he bent, kissing the back of her neck, sending gooseflesh to all parts of her body. "Good morning, Grace. Merry Christmas."

* * * *

He took a deep breath, absorbing the faint, sweet scent of her lilac perfume. She froze in his arms, allowing his lips to nibble her before she came back to life. She giggled and batted at him. He backed away. *Not here and not now.* Grace took out eggs and milk.

"French toast!" she hollered into the living room.

"Want some help?" Jake asked.

"You know how to cook?" She rested her hand on her hip.

"Two sisters, remember?"

"They put you to work?"

"Yeah. Everybody helped with meals when I was growing up." Grace took out two packages of bacon and tossed them to Jake.

"Here. Know how to cook bacon?"

"It's my specialty," he joked.

Sarah flew into the kitchen. "Let's open presents, let's open presents," she begged.

"How about you get to open…uh…" Grace started.

"Two. Sarah gets to open two before breakfast?" Jake put in.

"Mom, Dad…can I open two presents before breakfast?"

The chaos had begun. Sarah opened two gifts then Grace and Jake whipped up breakfast while Cara and Grant sipped coffee and snuggled together on the sofa. After the meal was done, they attacked the gifts under the tree. Cara loved the cashmere sweater Grace gave her and the diamond earrings from Grant. Grace got an emerald pendant and matching earrings from Cara, a pair of fine fur-lined leather gloves from Grant, and a stunning gold bracelet from Jake.

"I can't accept this," she said, trying it on.

"Why not? We're friends." Grace shot a skeptical look at him.

"What? What did I say?" He raised his shoulders to prove his innocence.

"Keep the bracelet, Pookie, it looks so wonderful on you."

"Pookie?" Jake smirked and cocked an eyebrow. Grace smacked him lightly in the shoulder before she handed him her gift. He opened the small package, which contained a pair of gold cufflinks.

"For all your opening nights."

He leaned over and kissed her lightly. "Thank you. They're perfect."

All action in the living room stopped when he pressed his lips to hers. Grace blushed several shades of pink, but it had seemed the natural thing to do. *We're like two couples, celebrating the holiday together. If we lived together, this would happen all the time. Live together? Snap out of it, man!*

Used to be, simply the concept of living with a woman, any woman, gave him a rash. When he thought about living with Grace, he panicked for a second then calmed. He pointed to the ceiling. "Mistletoe."

Cara stared at him then glanced around the room. "I don't remember hanging all this mistletoe," she said, moving her gaze from sprig to sprig strung up around the apartment. Jake felt heat rush up his neck to his face. "I helped out a little."

Grace's mouth fell open as Grant snickered, then said, "Very resourceful, Jake."

Jake's cell rang. His family was calling to thank him for the presents he had mailed and to reconnect. He took the phone into the hall where he had a lively, if brief, conversation with everyone, including his niece and nephew, before he had to dress. A heavy sigh escaped his throat as he hung up. *Never thought I'd miss them so much.*

He leaned back against the wall for a moment to recover his holiday cheer before rejoining the others. He wiped one eye with the heel of his hand and pasted a smile on his face. He noticed Grace watching him when he returned and wondered what she thought. *Probably thinks I'm a wimp. A sissy because I miss my family. Maybe I am.*

While the others cleaned up, Cara and Jake left for the theater. After the matinée, the rest of the day seemed to fly by. Wading through piles of discarded wrapping paper, cooking, and helping to straighten up were always holiday activities in his house. This year he did the same things with different people. *They're a family just like my family.*

Grace and Cara's obvious affection for each other was the cement that glued them all together. While he dreaded missing Christmas in Willow Falls, this had proved to be the next best thing.

That evening, he and Grace roasted a turkey and added leftover side dishes from the night before to fresh stuffing to make a mouth-watering buffet. Sarah was so worn out she lost her temper and had to take a time out to calm down. Grace flitted from one family member to another, perhaps to avoid him.

He packed up, thanked everyone, and headed for the door at about ten o'clock. Grant and Cara were doing dishes, and Sarah was in bed. Grace walked with him to the hall. *I don't think I made any progress with her.* Disappointment enveloped him like a gray fog. His shoulders sagged.

"Why so down? Missing your family?" Grace leaned against the wall.

"Being with your family was almost like being with mine."

"They're wonderful, aren't they? I'm very lucky," she beamed.

"Yeah. I was hoping you and I..." Courage failed him.

"You and I what? Didn't used to be a 'you and I,' but maybe there is one now?"

Hope welled in his chest. "You think?"

"Maybe."

"Want to go out New Year's Eve?"

"You don't have a date for New Year's?" she teased.

"Do you?"

"I do now."

"Oh. That's too bad." His spirits sank to the floor.

"With you, silly." She chucked him under the chin.

"Me?"

"Didn't you just ask me?" She rubbed his cheek lightly with her hand. "Ooh, I like you scruffy."

"So that's yes, then?"

"How many ways do I have to say it? Yes. But I promised to babysit Sarah. Cara and Grant are invited to some fancy shmancy party. I said I'd stay with Sarah. You can come over, and we can have champagne here. Would that be okay?"

"Hell, yeah! I'd much rather stay in than go out on New Year's anyway." *Maybe we can make love.* "Have to be after the show."

"You're performing on New Year's?"

"Yeah. New Year's Eve and a matinée on New Year's Day."

"That sucks."

"Not if I'm with you after." He combed his fingers through her silky hair.

Jake switched his hand to the back of her neck, gently easing her toward him. He lowered his lips to hers. She didn't resist, but softened against him. Jake dropped his packages and scooped her into his arms. Passion flowed through his body as he held her tight and ravaged her mouth.

A soft moan from her throat told him all he needed to know. He stepped back, his gaze seeking hers. He stared into blue eyes smoky with desire. "I wish we were somewhere more private," he breathed.

The ringing of his cell ruined the mood like a splash of cold water. It was Gunther Quill. "Merry Christmas, Gunther. What's up?"

"Did you see that scathing review of *Just In Time?*"

"I did. What a bitch! I'd love to know who Movie Maven really is."

"I was calling to see if you knew who she was."

"Nope. But if I find out, you'll be the first to know."

"I'll fix her. If I find out who she is, I'll ruin her. No one attacks Gunther Quill and gets away with it."

"Let me know. I might like to take a swing at her, myself." Jake chuckled.

"Merry Christmas, Jake. And don't worry. We're not paying any attention to her nasty review."

"Good. Goodnight." He closed his phone. "Gunther actually thought I knew who the bitch is who wrote that awful review. Wish I did." He looked up to see Grace standing stiffly a few feet away, eyes wide, face pale, frowning. "He sure spoiled the mood, didn't he?"

She nodded.

"Don't worry, honey. We'll get it back on New Year's. You and I have chemistry to burn," he whispered. He leaned down to give her a quick kiss and felt how rigid she was. "You okay?"

"Fine. See you on New Year's."

"Yeah and at the theater, too right?"

"Right."

"Merry Christmas, Gracie." Jake turned and headed for the elevator, humming "Jingle Bells."

Chapter Five

> *Black Magic should be titled No Magic. Yes, another time-waster. Mistaken identity and paranormal elements left me yawning. The dialogue was the worst I've seen since...oh, yes, last week!*

Gracie wrote another nasty write-up. Tiffany put it first among her reviews.

Research showed forty percent of readers were heading straight for the column. Her agreement with Tiffany kept her from posting each opinion on her blog, but she didn't care. She was getting paid, and the reviews were getting raves.

But the nasty comments were getting harder and harder to write as she began to feel very guilty about ruining sales for others in the same industry. *How would I feel if someone wrote something like this about my movie? I'd be crushed.* She tried to soften her sharp remarks but Tiffany rejected those columns and refused to pay her.

By New Year's, she had decided to cancel her arrangement with Tiffany. But she was the only person who knew the secret identity of the Movie Maven. Grace was afraid the cold-hearted editor would expose her. It was a dilemma.

She decided not to think about it on New Year's. She left the theater early to play a board game with Sarah before the child went to bed. Grant was getting ready for the party. Grace had made a few delicacies earlier in the day to share with Jake.

After reading Sarah a bedtime story, Grace set out a platter with cold jumbo shrimp and cocktail sauce, egg rolls from her favorite Chinese restaurant, stuffed mushrooms, and bacon-wrapped concoctions from a secret family recipe. Another dish held giant strawberries dipped in chocolate, cannoli, and mini napoleons from the French bakery down the street along with her own homemade chocolate chip cookies.

Grace's mouth watered while she arranged the food artfully. Grant entered the kitchen. "It's black tie tonight, and Cara said you tie a mean bowtie. Would you mind? Hey, what's all this?"

"No problem," Grace said reaching up. "A little something for Jake and me after the show."

"I think maybe I'm going to the wrong party. This looks great."

"Help yourself, I have tons." He nabbed an egg roll while Grace expertly wound the tie into a perfect bow.

"Jake's a lucky guy." He picked up a shrimp and carefully dipped it in cocktail sauce.

"He's got a good appetite."

"I mean, dating you."

She smiled with pleasure at his compliment. "Think so?"

"Sure do. You're one in a million, Grace. And that's not just because you're Cara's sister."

"Although that doesn't hurt, eh?"

"You two broke the mold."

"Done!" She pulled the bow tight. Grant took another shrimp and popped it in his mouth as he sought out the mirror in the dining room. "Cara was right. This is perfect. Thanks."

After a quick shower, Grace slipped into a turquoise velour, scooped-neck top and matching pants. Leaving her hair loose, she applied light makeup and her lilac cologne. She was ready for Jake, who'd be arriving with Cara any time now. Grant paced in the living room, checking his watch frequently. He looked up when she joined him. "It's ten forty-five. We need to get there before midnight."

"They should be here soon."

"Times Square will be a madhouse. I hope it doesn't stop traffic on Fifty-Third Street."

Before Gracie could reply, the door opened and Cara breezed in with Jake right behind her. "I'm so sorry, darling. Traffic was abominable. Bobby's waiting for us downstairs. I've got to change. Only be a minute." She stopped to kiss him before she disappeared into the bedroom. Grant joined her.

Jake handed Gracie a bag with a bottle of cold champagne in it, pink roses, a generous box of Fleur de Lis chocolates, the most expensive French confections in all of Manhattan—plus a copy of the romantic movie, *New Year's Eve*. He brushed her lips with his.

"Happy New Year, Gracie," he said, while taking off his down jacket and hanging it on the coat tree. She took the bag into the kitchen and brought out the platters she had prepared, placing them on the coffee table.

"What's all this?" he asked.

"Just some nibbles while we watch the movie." His eyes lit up as he sampled the shrimp then the stuffed mushrooms.

"Did you make these?"

She nodded. "I bet they taste as good as they look," she said, her eyes twinkling.

Jake sputtered and coughed, choking on a morsel of food. Grace pounded him on the back while she laughed. His face turned red and finally his throat cleared.

"That wasn't funny," he wheezed.

"I thought it was. Should have timed it *after* you'd finished."

"Ya think?" A smile crossed his lips.

"Can't forget a great line like that."

"I wish you would."

"I bet you do." Her eyes teased him.

"You're an amazing woman." Jake said as he followed her into the kitchen. They brought out the chocolates and champagne. Jake popped the cork and poured, while she set up the movie.

Before long, Cara came out dressed to kill in a low-cut, floor-length black velvet dress with long sleeves. She wore the diamonds Grant had given her for Christmas. The two couples bid each other Happy New Year, and then Grace and Jake were alone. They settled comfortably on the sofa with a hand-crocheted red, orange, gold and black afghan spread over their knees.

Gracie burrowed into his shoulder as he draped his arm around her. Jake's attention wandered during the movie. He focused on Grace, instead. Playing with her hair, planting kisses on her hand, then moving higher until he'd captured her full attention. She paused the movie when his lips sought hers, giving her mouth up to his. Jake appeared to be in no hurry, slowly exploring her with his tongue.

As the kissing got intense, he eased her back down until he was on top of her. Grace wound her arms around his neck then slid her hands into his hair. When he released her mouth, he began his gentle assault on her neck. Tiny kisses from her earlobe to her shoulder made her shiver. Her breath became ragged. He slipped his hand under her top and up her ribcage.

"You're not gonna slug me, are you?" He whispered in her ear as he closed his fingers around her breast.

"Uh uh," she mumbled as his touch sent fire sizzling through her. He wasn't grabby like he had been the night of the premiere, but gentle and loving instead. He massaged her, taking his time seeking her peak through her bra. Gracie relaxed, allowing the sensations he was creating in her body to take over, shutting down her mind. He kissed her more aggressively.

As he lay atop her, his arousal evident, she arched up into him. He nuzzled her neck, moaning her name. Grasping his shoulders, she hooked her leg around his waist. His fingers closed around her thigh and started to slide up when a cold breeze and a quiet gasp let them know they were no longer alone. Grant and Cara had returned.

The lovers separated in the blink of an eye. Grace smoothed her clothing and straightened her hair with her hands. Jake sat back against the sofa, pulling the afghan across his lap to hide his erection. The would-be lovers wiped their mouths. A snickering chuckle from Grant carried through the hall where the discreet couple waited for a few moments.

Cara coughed and lowered her eyes as she entered the living room. "Sorry. Didn't occur to me to call when we left the party," she said.

"It's okay. No harm, no foul." Grace tossed her hair.

Jake cleared his throat and took a sip of his champagne. "We have champagne left if you'd like to join us."

"Thanks, Jake, but it's already one thirty, and we have a show tomorrow. Goodnight." Cara and Grant went into their bedroom and closed the door.

"Oh. Right." He pushed to his feet. Grace followed. Alone in the hall, he pulled her up against him. "Did we almost make love?" he asked.

"A make-out session. Nothing to get bent out of shape about." She avoided his stare.

"I see," he said, nodding, but the gleam in his eye gave off a different message.

"Consider yourself lucky," she said, sliding her hands up his chest.

He pulled her closer with one arm while his lips kissed her right below her ear. "I do. Very lucky. I have a premiere next month in L.A. Come with me," he whispered.

"I do need to check on the house. You can stay in our guest room." She moved toward the front door.

"Guest room?"

"Is that a problem?" She cocked her head.

"Rather stay with you, but the guest room is my second choice."

"Don't push your luck," she said, grinning.

"I'm trying not to." He shrugged into his jacket while she opened the door.

"Thank you for the roses and chocolates."

"And thank you for the great food and…whatever." He tossed her a wicked grin.

"Happy New Year, Jake," Grace said, leaning in to kiss him. They indulged in a long embrace before separating. After the elevator scooped him up, Gracie returned to her room. Slipping between the sheets and pulling the down quilt up to her chin, she closed her eyes and dreamt about Jake for only a few seconds before she was asleep.

* * * *

The Liberty Connection is a disconnection. The plot is contrived, and the acting is wooden. They lost me in the first ten minutes, as the basic premise was so ridiculous.

I thought the movie was a comedy, a spoof of spy movies. Imagine how disappointed I was to learn the movie was the real thing…or tried to be.

Reviews kept getting shorter and harder to write. Tiffany pushed her to do more, and Grace resisted. Exasperated, Tiffany threatened to expose Grace if she didn't comply. So the nasty columns, no matter how hard they became, continued, and Grace regretted the day she sought revenge and made a deal with *Celebs 'R Us.*

Several days passed before she had time to stop and chat with Jake at the theater. She knocked on his dressing room door. When he opened up, she lazed in the doorway, shy about approaching him. He turned on the electric razor he held in one hand while motioning her in with the other.

Bare-chested, clad only in jeans, Jake moved to the mirror and continued shaving. Grace moved closer, fascinated. like a moth drawn to a flame. *What a sexy thing to do.* She wanted to run her finger down his cheek, following the path he was making.

"What's up?" he asked, making a face to pull his skin taut so the razor could do its job.

"Culture…" Her mouth went dry as her gaze slid down his body.

"What about it?" He shifted his grimace to shave his upper lip. Grace stared, her eyes riveted to his face.

"Museums…where there's culture. Wanna do a few museums?"

"Museums?" He ran his hand over his cheek.

I'll do that. She swallowed.

"Yeah, you know, the big ones, like the Met and the Modern. Then when someone brings it up in conversation, you'll…we'll know what they're talking about."

"Oh, like at the premiere? I'd like to forget that whole night."

"Makes two of us. Still, we should know about this stuff."

"Can't hurt." He turned to look at her. "Something wrong? You look…funny. Am I bleeding or something?"

Grace realized the heat she'd been sensing had become a blush, exposing her feelings. "I'm fine."

"You look like you're going to pass out," he said, pulling a chair close to her. "Sit down."

Gracie sank into it and took a deep breath. "Fine, really."

"Sure?" She nodded. "Start tomorrow?" She asked.

"Start tomorrow what?"

"The museum!" He nodded.

"Perfect. Pick me up at eleven." She pushed to her feet. He dropped a quick kiss on the tip of her nose and let loose his electrifying grin. It lit up the whole dressing room and the hallway outside, to boot. Gracie backed down the hall. Jake lounged in the doorway, filling it with his hunky, lanky frame. They stared at each other until Grace's ringtone broke the spell. It was her dancer friend, Dorrie. Jake went into his room and closed the door.

"Hey, Dorrie, what's up?"

"I'm in New York!"

"You are? Fabulous!"

"A friend who runs a dance studio sprained her ankle and asked me to fill in for her. So I'm teaching a ballroom dance class...and I'm begging you to come and sign up."

"Ballroom dance? Jazz is more my style."

"I know, but I need to fill this class. We're going to have a contest at the end. It's just for a few weeks."

"Do I need a partner?"

"Don't tell me a hot chick like you doesn't have a guy in New York?"

"Well, I sort of do, but I don't think he's a dancer."

"Bring him along. We'll teach him. It's going to be fun. Pleeaassee..."

"Okay, okay. I suppose an hour of exercise once a week wouldn't hurt."

"It's every day, starting next week. Intense. I'll email you the stuff."

"Okay. I'll see what he says."

"It'll be good to see you. How's that hamstring?"

"All better."

"Good, now I can give it a workout. Can't wait to meet your guy."

"He's not really my guy...sort of a friend."

"With benefits?"

"Just a friend."

"Oh. Too bad. See you next week." Grace joined Cara in time to fix her hair. "I'm going to take a ballroom dance class with Dorrie."

"She's here?" Cara applied lipstick.

"Yep."

"Partner?"

"Gonna ask Jake. Think that's a good idea?"

Cara turned to face her. "That's a great idea. He needs to know how to sing and dance. He's got the singing down, now the dancing!"

"Dorrie'll teach him."

"You'll teach him, Pookie." Grace finished combing out Cara and scurried into the wings to take her seat and watch the play for what seemed like the millionth time. *Never get tired of watching her act and getting a ton of applause. Not so bad watching Jake, either. He's really good.* She sat back in her folding chair with her bottle of water and turned her gaze to the stage.

When the show was over, Grace hung back, waiting to talk to Jake. As he came down the hall, she grabbed his arm. "Hey…"

"Hey." He cocked an eyebrow. "Something that can't wait until tomorrow?"

"Uh, yeah. Sort of. A friend of mine is teaching ballroom dancing here for a few weeks and wants me to take the class. I used to dance. And I need a partner…how about you?" The words came out in a rush.

"Wait a minute. You want me to take dance lessons with your friend?'"

"Not ballet or anything. Ballroom."

"You want me to be your partner in a ballroom dance class?"

"Yep. Cara says if you want to be a good actor, you have to know how to sing and dance. Since you already have the singing nailed…"

A slow grin spread over his face. "Hmm, getting close to you for an hour? Count me in."

She jumped up and down. "Great! Dorrie will be thrilled." *Are you the nicest man on Earth?*

"See you tomorrow at eleven." He leaned over for a quick kiss goodbye and was gone in a flash.

Cara peeked out. "Well?"

"He said 'yes'!"

The Brewster sisters linked arms and laughed their way down the hall and into Bobby's waiting limousine.

* * * *

It was unusually warm for a day in January as Grace and Jake strolled through Central Park on their way to the Metropolitan Museum of Art. Grace read from some pages she had printed out. "Where do you want to start, paintings, sculpture, armor, Egyptian mummy stuff, furniture?"

"You pick."

"I don't know what you're interested in."

"'Bout time you found out..." He grinned at her, and her insides melted. *Why do I like him so much?*

He laced his fingers with hers. "Let's just wander around."

"Okay." His grip was strong, warming her small gloveless hand. The sun brightened up the bare, gray tree limbs whose color matched the gray path winding through the park. It wasn't long before they spotted the back of the museum, rising majestically on the Fifth Avenue side. The huge, slanting wall of glass was unmistakable.

"Holy crap! That's one big museum," Jake said. He stopped and pulled her in close as he wrapped his arm around her shoulders.

After entering and obtaining two maps of the imposing structure, they spent most of the morning trying to find their way around and getting lost repeatedly. A quick game of hide 'n seek among the tombs of Egypt had Grace giggling and the other patrons shooting them nasty looks.

Jake treated Gracie to lunch in the cafeteria then they returned to the West Side. As they wended their way home on the twisty path, Grace brought out a small bag of peanuts in shells and stopped a few times to feed hungry gray squirrels. Jake rifled a few to the more timid squirrels, who hung back in the safety of large tree trunks.

As they neared the entrance to Central Park West, he drew her to him and planted a kiss on her lips. "Thank you for today."

"But we spent most of the time getting lost and didn't see much."

"Yeah, but now we know where some stuff is and can come back."

"Tomorrow morning the dancing begins."

"Then let's come back the day after...oops, no, I have a matinée. Thursday?"

"You're on."

He walked her to her building, bowed a discreet goodbye, and proceeded to his own small apartment. Grace couldn't stop smiling. *Best date in years...maybe ever.* She was humming as she entered.

Cara stopped to stare. "You're in a good mood."

"Fun at the Met."

"Oh, right. Date with Jake. See? Told you he'd be good for you."

"Know-it-all!" Gracie tossed a throw pillow at her sister.

"Don't start a fight you can't finish," Cara said, a smile stealing over her face. "Come with me. Time to pick up Sarah."

"You go. I'm kinda tired." Grace retreated to her room and closed the door. Lying on her bed, she thought about her life. *Jake's changed. He's not that drunken, grabby guy he was. What happened? Maybe I didn't know him. I don't want to like him, but I do. What will I do if he finds out who I really am...what I've done?*

She shuddered as a feeling of sadness pushed out her warm ones from their date. *Once he finds out, it'll be all over.* Depression at the thought of losing his affection weighed her down. She closed her eyes to shut out the sense of loss she was dreading and fell asleep.

* * * *

A week later, Grace returned from her dance lesson with Jake. They had worked on the Viennese Waltz. Gliding across the floor in Jake's arms had been heaven. She had given up building a wall around her heart and began to let him in little by little. Then Cara dropped a bomb.

"You don't need to stay after the show tonight."

"Why not?"

"Gunther Quill is in town for a couple of days. He's stopping by to talk about a new movie he's producing."

Grace dropped a dish that she was carrying into the kitchen. It shattered on the floor. "Gunther Quill?"

"Gracie! Are you hurt?" The two women stooped down to clean up the broken china.

"I'm fine." But the fluttering in her stomach belied her statement. *He's going to be at the theater?* Queasiness filled her and she ran to throw up.

"Are you sick?" Cara asked, standing in the doorway of Grace's room.

She shook her head.

"You're not pregnant, are you?" Grace shot a hostile look at her sister. "Whew! Good. Maybe you ate something bad."

"I'll be okay, Cara. Give me a minute." Grace closed the door and willed away her tears. Her legs wobbled like *Jell-O*, forcing her to sink down on the bed. *I can do this. I will do this. I won't fall apart. What happened, happened, it's over. Done. Moving on. No one knows, and I have to keep it that way.*

Within an hour, the women were in the car, and Bobby was winding the vehicle through a snarl of rush hour traffic, transporting them to the theater. Gracie forced her hand to stop shaking so she could help Cara apply her makeup.

As she was walking to the refrigerator to get juice, Jake grabbed her arm and pulled her into his dressing room. "You look good."

"In a T-shirt and jeans?"

"Yeah." The glow in his eyes lit a small fire inside her. "We need to practice our waltz."

"I know. Dorrie has open time early in the morning."

"Early? Hard to rise early when I don't get home until eleven. How early?"

"Maybe seven?"

"Ouch!"

"Try it. Maybe on Monday?"

"My day off?"

"You want to be good, don't you?"

"I want to be great. I want us to win." He eased her closer, resting his hands on her waist. "Wish me luck tonight?"

"I wish you luck every night." She stood on tiptoe and kissed him. He pulled her up against him for a passionate kiss then angled his head to deepen it. Gracie couldn't breathe, her heart rate jumped, and heat traveled through her.

When she regained her senses, she pushed away gently. "Hey, save it for the audience." But her breath was ragged, and her face was flushed.

"You're beautiful when you've been well-kissed," he whispered. Grace reached up and touched his cheek with a finger then her palm. *Would you be so sweet if you knew who I really am and what I've done?*

"Grab pizza with me tonight?"

She nodded then glanced at her watch. "Break a leg. Almost curtain time."

Jake took a deep breath and shot her an easy grin before he strode out the door and into the wings. Grace took her usual chair and focused on the play, trying to forget that her nemesis, Gunther Quill, would be backstage after the show.

Two curtain calls. Not bad for a Thursday. Gracie stood ready with a bottle of water for Cara. Jake disappeared on the other side.

"What time is it?"

Grace glanced at her watch. "Ten fifteen."

"Oh, God, Gunther is probably already here!" Cara rushed down the corridor to her dressing room. Grace heard the familiar voice as soon as Cara opened the door.

"Give me a minute to change…" Cara said, leaving Gunther in the hall.

He peered at Grace like a mountain lion that has spotted an unsuspecting rabbit. She could see his eyes glow, even as she started to back up. "No problem, Cara. Take your time. I have all night."

The gleam of his white teeth visible in his mirthless smile gave her the chills. She retreated until she found herself on the empty stage. Crew members had scattered to return to their homes. It was deserted and quiet.

Gunther advanced toward her. "Well, well. Ms. Grace Brewster. You're looking very tempting tonight. I see a bare table…" With the grace of a panther, he moved nearer quickly. Grace froze, like a deer in the headlights. "If you could bend over it, we could renew our acquaintance."

Her mouth was as dry as cotton, her heart beat out of her chest. Gracie shook her head.

"Why not? I can relieve your tension...in no time at all. A few thrusts and you'll be screaming my name."

Grace stepped back, but there was no place to go and no one around. As he inched closer to her, she found her tongue. "Go away, Gunther." She held up one hand.

"Don't be like that. You're a tasty morsel, my dear. I'm just coming back for seconds." He continued to move toward her, his strides becoming longer as he closed the gap between them.

"Get away from me." She tried to add conviction to her shaking voice.

"I don't like to take 'no' for an answer." As soon as he was within five feet, he lunged at her, grabbing her upper arms in a vise-like grip. She struggled, trying to pull away, but he held fast. She squirmed, turning her face to escape his mouth, until she heard a familiar voice.

"Grace! Grace! Gracie, where are you?" Jake walked onto the stage and stopped cold. His face clouded over. "What are you doing, Gunther?"

"Trying to make love to this little bit, but she's playing hard to get."

"Get offa me!" Gracie said, twisting in his grip.

"Let her go!" Jake hollered, crossing to them in three long strides. As he approached, Gunther dropped his hands. Grace rubbed the place where his grip had been cutting off her circulation.

"Fine, fine. She wants to play little miss virgin...but she didn't before. No, this tasty girl came willingly into my arms in LA. Didn't you, Grace, dear? Maybe now you're playing with Jake, instead, eh?"

Gracie shrunk back, horrified. Jake looked at her, his eyes hard. "Is that true?"

She stood silently, her feet riveted to the floor, unwilling to lie to Jake, but unable to admit the truth. Jake put his hands on her shoulders and gave her a little shake. "Gracie?" She nodded once. The look of surprise and disappointment on Jake's face squeezed her heart like a fist. He turned away from her toward Gunther, who stepped closer to Grace.

"Leave her alone. 'No' means 'no'." Jake insinuated himself between Grace and Gunther, facing the man.

Another voice joined them. "Gunther! I'm ready now. Come, let's powwow." It was Cara, who wandered into the tense scene.

Suddenly, Gunther's hard, challenging look melted away, replaced by a placid, accommodating expression. "Ah, Cara. I'm coming."

Cara's frown increased when she spied Grace cowering behind Jake. "What's going on? Gunther, did you do something to Gracie?"

"Just a little misunderstanding. That's all. No worries, Cara, darling. Let's go." Gunther placed his hand under Cara's elbow and steered her toward her dressing room.

"Gracie?" Cara called over her shoulder.

"I'm fine. Go." Grace waved her sister on. When they were gone, Jake turned to face her. "Is what he said true?" His voice was low, calm, and very serious.

I'm losing him! But I can't lie. She nodded, blinking rapidly. He turned to leave, but she grabbed his arm. "Wait! There's more to it than that."

"There usually is. Unless you're just a slut..." She stepped back as his words stung her like a thousand bees. "But then if you were a slut, you'd have slept with me on that first date. Slept with that sleazebag, but not me." Jake shook his head slowly. "And he's engaged. Grace, who are you?"

"I made a mistake. He promised—" Emotion choked her.

"Oh, he promised? You slept with him as a payback? Whoa, lady. Slut it is!" He backed up.

"No, wait. It's not like that...I...I..." Tears, no longer contained, cascaded down her cheeks. *Don't leave me.* She could see him soften a little. "Please don't leave. Please. Let me explain. I was stupid. He, he...please." Sobbing into her hands, Grace thought her heart would break until a pair of strong arms enveloped her. Peeking up, she saw concern and questions in Jake's eyes.

Resting her head on his chest, she continued to cry softly. *It's going to come out now. Maybe not all of it...but some. I can't stop. Can't leave him with lies.*

"He was forcing himself on you. I saw that." He pulled a handkerchief out of his back pocket and handed it to her. She wiped her nose and eyes before clutching the white material in a desperate grip.

"Can I tell you? Can we find somewhere quiet to go?"

"Yeah. The pizza place two blocks up has a backroom. It's almost always empty."

They headed toward the door until Gracie skidded to a halt. "Wait! My coat is in Cara's dressing room. Gunther is in there. I don't want to see him."

"I'll get it. What color?"

"Dark rose."

"Rose?" He smiled. "Uh...what's rose, red?"

"Sorry. Dark pink."

When they reached Cara's door, Jake knocked. Cara opened it and shot a questioning look at Grace. "Are you all right, Pookie?"

Grace avoided her gaze and stared at the ground. "I'm okay."

"Came to get her coat. We're going for pizza." Jake pushed into the small room, his eyes searching for the jacket. He retrieved it and shot an angry look at Gunther, who shrugged. Jake held it out for Gracie. "We won't be late, Cara," Jake said, taking Grace's hand and pulling her toward the exit.

"Later, Pookie," Cara called.

* * * *

Grace folded her fingers around Jake's as they walked, but he slipped his hand away from her and put it in his jacket pocket. His action was like a small, sharp knife jabbing her. *If he doesn't believe me, then why is he coming to listen to my side?*

Two slices of pizza with a beer for Jake. Only a glass of wine for Gracie. When she was upset, her appetite disappeared. While he ate, she sucked in air and blew it out, organizing her thoughts.

"I feel you hanging back, removed...suspicious. Why are we here?"

"Truth? You gave me a second chance after I behaved like a jerk on our first date. Thought I ought to hear you out before we split."

Her breath caught in her throat, and her heart stopped beating. *Before we split?* The sting behind Gracie's eyes alerted her that tears threatened, but she blinked rapidly to force them away. *I will not manipulate him with tears.* She clasped her hands together to keep them from shaking. *He's going to dump you, so what? If you're not in love with him, why does it hurt so damn much?*

After taking a gulp of wine for courage, Grace began her story, starting with the suggestion from Skip that she send her manuscript to Gunther.

"And you didn't know he was engaged?" Jake trained a cool eye on her.

"I always check for a wedding band, first. Then look on a man's desk for a portrait of his family. Gunther didn't have one picture of his fiancée, of any human being at all." She played with a napkin.

"He seduced you? Really? You want me to believe that kinda thing still happens?" Jake tilted back in his chair.

"I was naïve…okay, maybe just plain stupid. He said he'd read my script, and I've worked so hard…and waited so long to have my shot. So I believed him. Cara's a huge success, but I can't seem to even get started," she said, blinking rapidly again to stave off the invasion of another gush of tears, her voice growing smaller.

"All I wanted was a shot, a reading. No promise to make a movie out of it. Just a chance. The script is good. It'd have sold itself, Skip said so. I expected Gunther to say he'd read it, at least the treatment, maybe then the script. But he didn't…had no intention…instead I got…duped, betrayed, lied to…and yeah, seduced."

Grace stared at her hands, afraid to see a cold expression on his face. She heard him put down his beer but still didn't look up. He reached over and lifted her chin with a finger. She couldn't avoid his stare and looked back with as much confidence and defiance as she could muster, which wasn't much.

"You traded your body for a shot."

"Yeah. I'm not proud of it. It was a mistake, but…yeah. Haven't you ever slept with anyone, then regretted it?" Her gaze searched his.

"Yeah, but I never traded sex for…a favor or anything. Just a bad choice of partner."

"You're a guy. It's different."

He kept his eyes trained on her, his face solemn. Grace slipped her arms into her coat and finished the last of the wine in her glass.

"I'll be going..." she pushed back her chair but before she could stand, he clamped his hand down on her wrist.

"I'm not finished."

"Oh?" She cocked an eyebrow at him. "Whatever you have to say, I've said to myself a thousand times. Thanks for the wine, but it's late. I've got to get home. Nice knowing you." But Jake's iron grip held her fast. *Please let me go with some shred of dignity.*

"You're not leaving."

"Why draw this out? You pegged me. Slut. Please let me go." Tears could no longer be denied and slipped past her defenses.

He reached out with a paper napkin and wiped her cheeks. His hand cupped her chin. "Not a slut. A victim." He shook his head. "Gunther...that rat bastard, liar...lowlife! Fucking asshole." He muttered so low, Grace almost couldn't hear it. "I'm sorry this happened...and that you were afraid to tell me."

He believes me?

He raised his gaze to hers as he took her hands and pulled her around the table to him. She crawled into his lap, and he closed his arms around her tight. She sobbed into his chest as he kissed her hair. In a minute she calmed down, snuggling her face into the hardness of his pecs and the softness of his flannel shirt. She inhaled deeply of his scent, mixed with a whiff of piney aftershave. The warmth of the fabric against her cheek soothed her. *Can I stay like this forever?*

He sighed. "What am I going to do with you?"

"I'm incorrigible. I know. Stay with me?" She tried, unsuccessfully, to keep the note of hope out of her voice.

"That goes without saying." He stroked her hair.

"Does it?"

He looked down at her. "Of course. Look, you were naïve, I was a jerk, and Gunther was worse. Granted, different situations, but let's forget both. Agreed?"

She reached up and pulled his head down until their lips met. "Thank you," she whispered.

"Don't thank me. I'm not doing you a favor," he said into her mouth.

"Shut up." She kissed him hard.

"Eh, buddy, get a room. This is a public place." A man wearing a long dirty white apron and pushing a broom gestured to the door.

Jake chuckled, helped her up, and put on his coat. They left. Jake put Grace in a cab. "Until tomorrow at eleven." She reached through the window to touch his face and smiled.

* * * *

"It's times like this when I wish I smoked," Cara said to Grant as she paced in the living room.

"Why wouldn't Grace tell you if something terrible happened to her?" He was sitting on the sofa cradling a small snifter of brandy. Cara took a sip from her glass then put it down. "I don't know. She's always come to me when she was in trouble."

"But she has Jake now. Maybe you'd better get used to her leaning on him more than on you."

Cara snapped her attention to him. "She's not married to him. Hell, as far as I know, she doesn't even like him much."

"Really?" He raised his eyebrows. "She gives a damn good imitation of a woman in love, if you ask me."

"Love?"

"Yep. I ought to know what a woman in love looks like," he chuckled.

"Oh my God," she sank down on the sofa next to him. "I think you're right. Gracie has never disliked anyone as much as Jake. It must be love."

"Whoa, what?"

"Of course. Makes sense. When she really dislikes a guy, she doesn't talk about him. It's like he doesn't exist. But when she's ranting about him, then I know he's broken through her defenses and gotten under her skin."

"She hasn't stopped criticizing him and making fun of him when he's not around."

"Must be major love," Cara said, a small grin tugging at her lips.

The door opened, and Grace tiptoed down the hall to her room. Cara pushed to her feet and called out in her best stage voice, "Ah, ah…no, no, I don't think so. Get in here, Miss Pookie,"

Grace looked up, stunned. "Didn't know you guys were still up."

"You don't think I can go to sleep after what happened…whatever it was…in the theater tonight, do you? Explanation. Now!"

Grace walked slowly into the living room and sat down. "What do you want to know?

Cara narrowed her eyes. "I want to know what's going on, that's what. The truth. All of it. Now!"

Chapter Six

The roar of the engine as the plane taxied down the runway had always thrilled Grace. This time, with Jake settled next to her in first class, her heart was thumping with excitement that had nothing to do with the take-off.

Staying in the house together. No interruptions. Jake closed his fingers over hers as the silver bird lifted off the ground. Happiness soared through her. . *Still can't believe he doesn't hate me for Gunther.* Afraid to make her wishes more concrete by thinking about them, imagining a future with Jake, she pushed those thoughts out of her mind. *Focus on the weekend. A weekend with Jake. Be happy with that. Make it be enough.*

Snuggling down into her seat, she squeezed his hand. He turned to face her. "Scared?"

"Love flying."

"Me, too."

She studied his face, the night's growth of beard, the fullness of his lower lip, the brown hair falling onto his forehead. Warmth spread from her middle to her lower region as she shifted her gaze to his long and agile fingers.

She remembered the feel of them closed around her breast and her breath began to quicken at the thought of them caressing other parts of her body. Even imagining them unbuttoning a blouse or unzipping her jeans made her chest heave a bit. She chewed on her lower lip in an attempt to cool herself down but was unsuccessful.

"We'll be alone at your house?"

"Cara's house? Yes."

"Good." A steamy glance from him made her skin prickle in anticipation of his touch.

She returned his smoldering smile, causing him to lean in and kiss her. The soft, lingering pressure of his lips on hers added fuel to the fire simmering inside her. She cupped his cheek, running her thumb down his face.

"Sorry. I didn't shave this morning. Giving my skin a break."

"Love this. You wear scruffy well."

The plane leveled off and the cabin attendants came around offering champagne. They asked Jake for some autographs, and he was happy to oblige. "Autographs. Never thought that would happen." He laughed and gave his head a shake. "My sisters would make sure my head didn't swell over this."

"I can do the same if you like," Grace offered.

"No thanks. Like you just the way you are."

Do you? Could kiss you for that. I feel the same about you.

When the bubbly wine arrived, they toasted to each other and sipped.

"I hope this premiere goes better than the first."

"I hope you're happy with your performance in this one."

"God, if I messed up, Movie Maven will probably be there to announce it to the world."

No, she won't. Grace squeezed his hand. "Don't worry about her. You'll be fine. We'll have fun at the party, and go swimming. Our pool is heated."

"A heated pool? Didn't bring my suit."

"Maybe you don't need one," she shot him a sexy grin that lit up his eyes.

He lifted his eyebrows. "Really?"

"You can always swim in your boxers…after all, it's just us."

"Oh. Thought you had something else in mind." His crestfallen expression made her laugh. "Were you teasing me?"

"You'll have to wait to find out."

He sat up straighter in his seat. "If I'm in my boxers, what'll you wear?"

"I told you…wait and see."

"Filet Mignon or Shrimp Scampi?" The stewardess interrupted their charged conversation to take their request for lunch. After eating, Jake pulled a manuscript out from his carry-on bag under the seat.

"More scripts to read?" Grace asked.

"Yours." Her eyes widened. "Perfect to read now." He opened to the first page. Grace buried her nose in a book, afraid to watch his reaction, but sleepiness caused her to slip a bookmark in, rest her head on Jake's shoulder, and close her eyes. When she awoke, the plane was descending. She peeked out the window to see the sprawl of L.A. below. Jake stretched and closed the screenplay. "Almost there," he muttered.

"What do you think?" He shot her a quizzical glance. "About the screenplay, of course!"

"Oh! Yeah. I love it."

"You do?" She couldn't keep a note of desperation out of her voice.

"It's fresh. Original. You have an amazing ear for dialogue."

Pleasure brought heat to her face and a smile to her lips. "Thank you. That means a lot."

"I mean it. You know me well enough to know that my brain doesn't always filter my words. If I didn't like it, I couldn't hide it from you."

"Nice, juicy part for the right, hot leading man."

"Quinn would be great. Think he'd do it?"

"I was referring to you!"

"Oh!" He laughed as an attractive blush stained his cheeks. She slipped her hand in his, holding tight until the seatbelt sign was turned off. A car awaited them and before long they were wending their way up Benedict Canyon Drive. The lights on the house were lit by a timer to help keep thieves away. Grace fumbled with her key in the lock, nervous yet excited at the prospect of Jake sleeping in the house with her. He carried their luggage inside.

"This is your room," she said, turning on the light in the guest bedroom. "I'm down here."

Jake dropped his bag first then carried hers to her room. "This is a beautiful house. My first mansion." He looked around at the white walls, colorful tile floors, some in turquoise and green, and others in tones of orange and brown.

"Don't know if I'd call it a mansion. There are many here much larger than ours."

Opening the sliding glass door to the terrace, Grace took Jake's hand and led him outside. Chaise lounges were stacked three and four deep. The glass top table sported a closed umbrella and four white wrought iron chairs.

"Wow," he said. "What an ideal place to skinny-dip." A musical sound alerted them. Jake checked his phone then his watch. "Car will be here for us in an hour."

"An hour? Oh my God!"

Forty-five minutes later, Grace stood with her back to Jake, holding her dress closed. "Please zip…then I'll tie your tie."

"You know how to do that?" He asked, while he found the zipper on her shimmery sky-blue jersey, floor-length dress.

"I'm an expert. Ask Grant." Gracie took several deep breaths to calm herself as the tingle from his fingers on her bare back traveled through her. *God, I want him.* Her eyes closed as she focused on the feeling he created inside her. He kissed her shoulder gently.

"Not like I wouldn't like to keep…better finish," he mumbled, pulling the zip up all the way. Gracie adjusted her breasts into the cups sewn in the dress before turning to him. "Wow! You look even better with the dress closed up." His gaze slid down her body like the caress of a warm hand.

"You say the sweetest things."

"Words…not my strong suit. Actions…ah, there I shine." His eyes glittered with lust.

He looked so sexy with his hair falling over his forehead and his tie hanging loose, waiting for her to work her magic. *This is what he'll look like when he's getting undressed. When we get home tonight.* A small shiver raced up her spine. "Closer," she motioned.

"Don't have to ask me twice." He stepped up until his chest was only an inch from hers. She swallowed before reaching up and grasping both ends of his bowtie. A few seconds later, it was tied. "Always wear a tux. It suits you."

"Oh? Should I wear it to bed? Making love? Swimming?"

She burst out laughing. "Tuxedo pajamas!"

Now it was his turn to chuckle. He leaned down to kiss her. "Thank you," he said, feeling the tie.

A honk from the driveway diverted their attention. Grace grabbed a gauzy shawl and followed Jake to the door. He opened it with a flourish and, sweeping his arm through the air before her, said, "Your chariot awaits, m'lady."

"Not good with words. I get it," she snickered.

"Thanks a lot!"

"But looking forward to those actions you promised." She smiled at him.

"Makes two of us," he snickered as he closed the door behind them.

* * * *

As the car drew near the theater, Grace laced her fingers with Jake's. He turned to her.

"Don't worry. Gunther won't be here. Good thing, too. I might have to deck him for what he did to you." Anger flashed in his eyes.

"Let's forget him for tonight. Your fans are waiting. Slap on your sexy smile."

He pulled his lips back, showing his teeth. "How's this?" She laughed and he joined her, so that when the door was opened, he wore a genuine smile and merriment twinkled in his eyes. He offered her his hand, and they marched up the red carpet together. Fans went wild when they saw him and he grinned and waved in return.

Suddenly, Grace realized she was lucky to be with him. *Jake the movie star? Jake my friend and maybe lover.* His fame was growing, and before long, he might snag a movie series like Quinn or be lucky enough to get some great scripts, like Cara, and be blasted into the public eye twenty-four/seven. *Is that a good thing? For him, probably. For me? Doubtful.*

He leaned over to her, "Looks like more fans at this one than the last one. Guess Movie Maven didn't hurt my career." She let out a breath and squeezed his fingers. *Thank God!*

They settled into their seats. Jake laced his fingers with hers and rested their joined hands on his thigh, like he did the last time. Grace relaxed and snuggled closer to him, scooting down to get comfortable. The lights dimmed, and the title came up on the screen, *Driving Force*. She whispered, "Break a leg." He raised her hand to his lips.

At the end of the movie, the applause was deafening. Grace breathed a sigh of relief. *He was good, really good.* She turned to him, a look of relief evident on his face. "You were amazing."

"Really?"

"Really," she said.

They stood up as the director and one of the executive producers approached. They slapped him on the shoulder as murmurs of "fine job," "well done," and "excellent" were bandied about. Jake beamed under their praise. A sense of pride in him welled up inside of Grace, confusing her. *Why am I proud of him? He's not mine. Just a friend or maybe a brief affair…right?*

The limo whisked them away to a huge party at Limoges West on Rodeo Drive. Jake helped Grace out of the car and tucked her arm through his.

"Are you going to desert me for the first available female that comes along?"

"Did I.?"

"You certainly did!"

Jake's face flushed. "I'm sorry. Seems like I keep saying that to you."

"What?"

"Apologizing."

"We agreed to forget that night, right?" Grace cozied up to him, gripping his lapels.

"Yeah. That's right."

She tilted her head up and kissed him. "That ought to send a message to the women here."

Jake grinned. "Want a Cosmo?" He spotted the bar and led her over. Grace glanced around the room, seeking a table of food, but found none.

"Take it easy with those," she warned him as he took a gulp.

A waiter balancing a tray of *hors d'oeuvres* stopped by. Grace plucked two cheese puffs off the tray, stuffing one in Jake's mouth and one in her own. Then she snatched two mini quiches before the server moved on. "Eat," she said. "Or you'll get loaded…and do something stupid."

Starlets, producers, and cast members stopped by to congratulate Jake. Although she tried to hold on to him, they got separated. Grace consoled herself with a second Cosmo and food from a buffet she found hiding in another room. She made a plate for Jake, but he seemed to have disappeared.

She wandered out on the back deck just in time to see him easing out of the embrace of some young woman she didn't recognize. She stopped to watch as he grasped the woman's upper arms and moved her back, away from him. Grace let out the breath she didn't even realize she was holding when she noticed his uneasy smile and the look of disappointment on the young woman's face. *Is he saving himself for me? Do I have his heart?*

Grace marched up to Jake and kissed his cheek before speaking, addressing her words to him but looking directly at the young woman. "Darling, here you are. I've been looking all over for you." She thrust the food at him.

"Grace, this is…I didn't catch your name?" Jake said, taking a cold shrimp.

"Never mind," the woman said, waving her hand and moving away.

Laughter bubbled up inside Gracie, and she couldn't contain it. "Did I save you?"

"Sure did. Thanks. What an octopus!" Jake straightened his tie and collar.

"How many Cosmos have you had?"

"Dunno. They sure are good." He munched on a green bean.

"Maybe we should go. Before something bad happens."

"Like what?"

"Like you make a pass at someone."

Jake put down the plate, took her in his arms and kissed her. "You're the only one I want to make a pass at."

"Are we going to have another scene in the limo like last time?" She pushed away from him.

"I hope not."

"Meaning?"

"Meaning you might not say 'no'?" he whispered in her ear.

She laughed. "If you paw me in the backseat, you'll get the same treatment."

"I'd never do that. I mean at home." He leaned down to kiss her neck.

"Oh, that's another story. You'll have to wait and see." Jake managed to down one more Cosmo before he agreed to bid his colleagues farewell and head home. He was pretty high, but not drunk like the last time. *Maybe his confidence is up after this movie. Or maybe because you're not being mean to him. Hey, I'm not responsible for him getting drunk. Glad he's not drunk now.*

In the car, Jake pulled Grace into his shoulder and they snuggled for the entire ride home. Once in the house, she toed off her shoes immediately, leaving them by the front door.

"Geez, you got short."

"Those shoes were killing me," she said, rubbing her foot.

"Can you swim at night?" Jake asked, pulling his tie until the bow came undone.

"Sure. Come on." Grace padded out onto the deck and switched on the light on the bottom of the pool then soft lights on the deck.

"That's so cool," Jake said, his gaze on the water shimmering in the light. "They change the color of the water." Grace pulled a chaise close to the edge. "It's romantic," he chuckled.

"Would you mind? Without heels, this dress is way too long. Besides, I want to get comfortable." Grace backed up to him.

"Unzip?"

She nodded. His long fingers took their time unzipping her. She clamped her arms to her sides to keep the strapless dress from falling. When he was done, he cupped his hands over her shoulders and kissed her neck. She shivered. "It's cold out here." She tried to cover up her response to him.

Jake took off his shoes and socks and dipped his toes in the water. "But the water is warm."

"I turned the heater up before we left. Figured you might want to swim in February."

She padded over to the chaise and turned, poised, staring at him. He stopped and returned her stare. Suddenly, she let go of her gown, which pooled at her feet, revealing her naked body. Jake swallowed. Sweat appeared on his forehead as his gaze raked her form. Grace took two steps to the side of the pool and dove in. When she surfaced, she motioned to Jake, who was already ripping his clothing off as fast as he could.

Standing on the edge, he dropped his boxers and dove in. He swam to her side, but she ducked underwater, swimming away. She led him on a merry chase. At one point, he was doing a speed-crawl when she came up behind him and smacked his bare behind. He stopped immediately. "This means war!" he hollered.

Grace's eyebrows shot up, and she tried to get away, but Jake was too fast for her this time. He lunged at her, his palm connecting with her head as he dunked her under water. She came up sputtering and laughing.

She was trapped in the corner of the shallow end while trying to swim backward as Jake zoomed across the pool, closing the distance between them in a matter of seconds. He reached his long arms out to prevent her escape. Slowly he moved closer, his gaze feasting on her nakedness, desire glittering in his eyes. "Does this mean 'yes'?"

She nodded, looking up at him. He lowered his head, his lips claiming hers in a hard, demanding kiss. He pulled her up against his wet chest with one hand while the other closed around her bare bottom. When he lifted her, she wound her legs around his waist and her arms around his neck.

"I want you," he whispered, his hand on her breast, massaging. "I want you bad."

She gasped for breath when his mouth lifted off hers. "Me, too." *Never wanted anyone like I want him. God, oh God. He's so beautiful.* Grace slid her palm down over the light brown hair on his firm chest. Her hands seemed to have a mind of their own as they wandered over his body, touching, caressing, feeling his hair, skin, and muscles. *He's all man. Gorgeous.* She peeked at his abs, nicely defined but not too much.

His stare burned a trail down her skin. He raised one foot to rest on a stair and seated her on his thigh. With his hands freed-up, he explored her body, starting with her chest then moving downward. With his face in her neck, he started to moan her name.

Grace leaned back and Jake immediately put his arm behind her to keep her from falling. He kissed his way from her neck to her chest, closing his mouth on her peak. Now it was Gracie's turn to moan. Her fingers gripped his shoulders, squeezing into his muscles as heat grew in her core.

Jake raised his head. "You're incredibly beautiful." Something tickled her, and she realized it was his erection. A giggle escaped her throat. "What?" He asked, his golden eyes rimmed with fire for her.

"You're ready…"

He chuckled. "Figured that out, eh?"

"I can feel it."

He laughed. "Then let's go. Need to get you up to speed." He picked her up as if she was a feather and carried her out of the pool, lowering her slowly onto the chaise. They both began to shiver in the sixty-degree chill and wrapped themselves in bath sheets they found stacked on a small table.

With her lips turning blue, Gracie took Jake's hand and led him into the master bathroom. The enormous shower stall had two shower heads on opposite walls. This water palace was tiled, floor to ceiling, in white tiles with beautiful designs painted on in light blue and lavender. She turned on both jets and within seconds a warming steam had filled the room.

"Join me," she said, stepping under the warm spray. Jake didn't hesitate.

"Ladies first," he said, grabbing the soap, lathering up, and spreading it over her body. Gracie smiled into his eyes as he caressed her with lavender-scented suds. His hands slipped over her skin, not missing an inch then settled between her legs. She soaped up his chest, then continued down until she closed her fingers around him. He was hard as granite.

"Rinse off. I can't wait much longer," he said, stroking her with an ever-increasing rhythm.

Grace bent her head back to rest against the tile and closed her eyes while warm water cascaded down on her. "Oh, God. Don't stop." Fire raged within her. Passion coiled up tighter and tighter as his fingers played her.

He supported her bottom with one hand while he slipped two fingers into her. As he pumped her, her hips moved in tandem with his hand. She groaned his name as she lost control. Jake lowered his lips to her neck and whispered, "Are you protected?"

Her eyes flew open as she shook her head. "It's okay, okay," he said, lowering her and stepping out of the shower. Jake grabbed a towel and wrapped it around his waist as he ran into his room to retrieve a condom. He was back in a flash. While he fiddled with the foil wrapper, Grace lowered herself and took him into her mouth.

"Holy Hell!" he said, dropping the packet as he braced himself against the shower wall.

Grace raised her head and smiled broadly at him. "Like that, do ya?"

"Where did you…?"

"Condom?" she interrupted. Jake bent over and retrieved the small package from the shower floor. In a few seconds, he'd covered himself and turned to Grace. He signaled her to come to him, then cupped her behind with his palms and lifted her up. She braced herself by holding onto his shoulders as he lowered her onto his erection.

The feeling of him entering her sent her pulse racing again. *Hot damn!* Her eyes closed as she gave herself over to him completely, softening in his arms. Jake balanced her with ease, moving her up and down, slowly at first then progressively faster and harder.

Their slippery bodies bumped then rubbed together, making her tingle. Arching her back pushed her breasts against his solid chest, exciting her more. His moan signaled his response to her hard nipples brushing his skin. Gracie heard their panting and soft groans over the sound of the water.

He's so strong, taking over… Her fingers sensed the tension building in his muscles as their passion grew rapidly with each thrust. Jake was no longer the shy, country boy who didn't know what to do. He was the masterful lover, taking her places she'd never been. His strength braced her, allowing her to let go in ways she never had before.

Within minutes, a powerful orgasm ripped through her, causing her head to fall to his shoulder, her lips to suck on his skin, and her nails to dig into his back.

"Jake…I…" Then speech failed her.

* * * *

Seconds later he called her name, hugged her tightly to him while he buried his face in her neck. Jake closed his eyes and saw sparks of color, like tiny fireworks, as pleasure shot through to every corner of his body. Making love to Grace had sent him beyond any previous experience. The satisfaction coursing through his veins also trickled into his well-guarded heart, bringing with it a sense of joy.

Loosening his vise-like grip, he cradled Grace in his arms as he regained normal breathing. He stroked her wet hair and kissed her cheek then her mouth tenderly. Opening his eyes to the stare of her large blues looking innocent and questioning, his heart squeezed. He held her in his grip, reluctant to let her go.

"Gracie...I..." he whispered. But the words of love he intended to utter caught in his throat. Jake didn't declare his love to women often. A sensation of vulnerability washed over him, suddenly he was naked with her in a way he'd never been naked before, and it wasn't comfortable. Slowly, he lowered her to the ground. She leaned in and placed her palm flat on his chest then planted a sweet kiss there.

She reached up and turned off one shower, and he turned off the other. Fresh, soft towels were wrapped around clean, sated bodies. A wall of embarrassment flew up between them. Grace blushed at her nakedness, covering herself quickly.

"It's late," she said. He turned toward his room, but she caught his hand. "Stay with me tonight?"

"Thought you'd never ask," he replied. *I never spend the night. Love 'em then home to sleep alone. Tonight I want to be with her.* They padded into her large, orchid-colored bedroom. She pulled down the covers on her queen-sized bed and got in, sliding over to make room for him. He followed, pulled the bed clothes up over them and inched closer to her.

She lay on her side, leaving room for him behind her. He moved up flush against her and draped his arm around her, pulling her in tight and securing her there.

"Do you always spend the night with women you have sex with?"

"Rarely...actually never."

"Oh?"

"I want to be here with you, together all night. Is that all right?"

"More than all right."

"Do you spend the night with guys...?"

"I don't sleep with a lot of men. I had one steady boyfriend for three years in college. He never wanted to spend the night. It was hard to find privacy at school anyway."

"What happened to him?"

"He took a job in Hong Kong, and that's the last I saw of him."

"Did he break your heart?" Jake stroked her arm.

"A little. Though I don't think I was in love with him. He was convenient. But my pride was hurt."

"I get it. His loss and my gain. I can't imagine making love to you and not wanting to spend the night."

A smile curved her lips. "I agree."

"So if I had made an excuse and escaped to my room, you'd have…"

"Broken your neck." She giggled.

Jake cuddled up closer, bending his knees to mirror hers. He moved to her neck and took a deep breath. "You always smell so good."

"Yeah?"

"Yeah. That first night in the limo…God. What were you wearing? The smell drove me wild."

"Oh, so it's my perfume's fault that you pawed me?"

"I thought we were forgiving and forgetting that incident."

"Oops. Right. Sorry." The couple melded together into a comfortable position. Grace broke the silence. "You were awesome tonight. Where'd you learn to make love like that? No, don't answer!"

"You're inspiring." He nuzzled her. "If we don't go to sleep, I'm afraid you might get me going, and I'd have to take you again here and now."

"Really?"

"How about in the morning?"

"Oh, yeah. Wake up sex."

"Almost as good as make-up sex."

"With you…just as good." He could hear the sleepiness in her voice.

He kissed her hair. "Sleep now, Gracie, honey."

"Hmm, yeah. Love you, Jake."

His breath stopped. *Did I hear right? Did she say she loves me?* But her even breathing told him he was too late to confirm what he heard. Grace was asleep. *Yeah, baby, I love you, too.* He closed his eyes and sleep came faster and easier than it had in months.

In the morning, Jake opened his eyes with the invasion of the sun and rolled over. To his delight, Gracie slept next to him, her long hair tangled, framing her face beautifully, her shoulder and one breast almost exposed. He rolled on his side, taking advantage of being the first one awake to study her.

His gaze traveled down her serene, lovely face to her chest. Slowly, he peeled the sheet down a little bit until more of her was bared. He devoured her flesh with his eyes, his fingers tingling to touch and his lips to kiss.

She stretched her arms above her head, gave off a little squeaking noise from her throat and her eyelids fluttered. A smile spread slowly across her face as she spied him staring at her. *Remember, she said she loved you. Confirm that? What if she denies it? Just shut up.*

"Morning."

"Morning," he replied. "You're beautiful when you sleep."

"Been watching me long?"

"Only a few minutes. Like Sleeping Beauty." Seemingly suddenly self-conscious, she covered herself with the bedclothes. "Don't do that," he said, easing them down again. "Let me look at you."

She lay still, a blush stealing up her chest into her neck. Reaching out, she combed his unruly hair off his forehead with her fingers. The gentle, loving touch soothed him. *She loves you. You love her, too. Tell her.* But the words wouldn't come as a wave of cold fear swept through him. She looked vulnerable, bringing him closer to confiding his feelings. *Start slow.*

"I've…uh…never felt like that with anyone before," he said.

"Really? Never…uh…come with a woman?" Her eyes widened, embarrassment heated her cheeks.

"Of course I have. Not that. The other…stuff, you know."

"Feelings?"

"Yeah. That stuff." He cast his gaze down.

"Never had feelings for another woman?"

"Not like I have for you."

"What kind of feelings?" She rested her palm on his shoulder.

"Made it all special…different than before."

"How?" She kept probing, but he was tongue-tied.

"Like something more." He glanced at her, then away again.

"More than what?"

"More than just sex." He closed his fingers over her hand.

"I hope so." she said.

"You know."

"You mean like love?"

"Yeah. Like...love."

"Are you trying to say you love me, Jake?" The heat of a flush spread over his face. She stroked his rough cheek. "I already said it, so you wouldn't be saying it first."

"You weren't like asleep when you said that?"

She chuckled, "Hardly. Don't say I love you in my sleep. Only awake."

He leaned in and kissed her. "I love you, too, Gracie."

She inched closer to him and he rested his hand on her back for a second before he ran his fingers up and down her smooth, silky skin. "God you feel good."

"So do you." She flattened her palm on his chest.

Her touch started a fire in him. He moved his hands to her breasts, enjoying free access to her body. Pressure between his legs told him he was already erect and ready. *Now to get her to the same level.*

Chapter Seven

Grace set tight controls on herself to keep from jumping up and down when Jake admitted loving her. She allowed a smile on her face, but no screaming or attacking him. It wasn't easy. Her heart seemed to swell to twice its normal size as it pounded a fast, steady rhythm.

He loves me? She decided not to question but just accept it. Besides crushes, she had never been truly in love before, and the sensation was heady. She stretched out, moving her body up against his, staring into his golden eyes, where adoration mixed with lust.

He kissed her long and slow. A sigh escaped her throat as she surrendered to his desire, her own bursting forth under his touch. He moved his lips down her neck to her chest where he made love to her breasts. Slipping his hand between her legs he whispered in her ear.

"I'm ready, but you're not. Wait a minute." His mouth slid to her abs and went lower and lower. When his head stopped between her legs, she sucked in a breath. "Oh my God!" she exclaimed when his tongue touched her tender flesh. He brought her to his level of arousal within minutes.

Twenty minutes later, Jake poised over her with one last groan before he collapsed. Gracie was still dreamy from the pleasure he had given her. She ran her nails gently over his back, which was lightly coated with sweat.

"Oh, baby," he muttered. "You're amazing." Gazing into his eyes, her heart filled with love for the shy, awkward man who could make love like nobody's business. Sex had been enjoyable for her in college but never an explosive, heart-stopping experience like it was with Jake.

"So this is what they're talking about," she murmured after he rolled off her and onto his side.

"What?"

"All the talk about how great sex is. I guess not with everybody."

"You didn't enjoy sex before? That's hard to imagine. You're so…so…responsive."

Heat came to her cheeks. "Thank you."

"No, really? Not like this before?"

She shook her head. "It was okay, but nothing like it is with you." He beamed. "I guess you're an expert."

Jake chuckled. "I don't like to brag, but I know my way around the bedroom."

"Guess you do. How many women have you had?" She raised herself up on an elbow and stared at him.

He paled. "Dunno."

"Just give me a general idea…hundreds? Thousands?" He went straight from ashen to beet red. "Thousands, really?"

"No, no."

"That's a relief."

"Enough. Does it matter?"

She shook her head. "Just yankin' your chain."

"Oh?" He cocked an eyebrow as a devilish gleam lit up his eyes. "How about this?" He launched into a tickle attack that had her screaming for him to stop and gasping for breath in no time. "That's what you get for asking that question." He grinned.

Grace lay back in the bed, sucking in air and calming down. "It's always the shy ones…"

"What?"

"Yeah. Always the shy ones who score the most. Women don't see 'em coming."

"You saw me coming."

"Hard to miss a Mack truck!" She fell into a fit of giggling.

"Oh, that's funny, huh? I'll show you funny," he said, pulling her across the bed and into his arms. Grace hooked her leg around his waist and accepted his hard, possessive kiss. "You're mine now, Gracie Brewster. All mine."

Her heart sang at his words, and her body melted into his. "Yes, sir. All yours."

Interrupted by the rumbling of her stomach, she disengaged from his embrace. "I'm starved. Breakfast!"

"Can I shower first?"

She nodded. "Meet me in the kitchen." After setting up the coffeemaker, Gracie put fire under the pan for eggs. She stood at the stove, turning bacon, wearing one of Cara's filmy, short negligées in blue. Jake, in jeans only, joined her. He came up behind her and embraced her.

She leaned back into him and shut her eyes for a second. The scent of him scrubbed clean mixed with the fresh aroma of soap and a slightly sweet aftershave. *Never smelled anything as good as Jake.*

"Bacon and eggs? My favorite." He kissed her hair.

"Mine, too."

Jake released her and searched the cabinets. Finding plates and utensils, he set the table for two then filled two mugs with coffee. "How do you take your coffee?" he asked.

"One sugar, light. Why?"

He prepared her drink and put it on the counter next to the stove. Winding an arm around her waist, he whispered, "I want to know everything about you. Even the little things."

She grinned. *Sweet! You can know everything, except Movie Maven.* The food was ready in no time. "Our first breakfast together," she said, picking up a piece of bacon.

"The first of many. I hope." He took a forkful of eggs.

"What do you want to do today?" The glint in his eye made her laugh. "I get it. But what else? We can't spend the whole day in bed."

"We can't?"

"It's beautiful outside. Let's drive down to the beach."

"It's too cold to swim."

"How about a picnic on the beach?"

"Perfect. Ever make love on the beach?"

She shook her head.

"Ah, there's always a first time. But be careful of the sand. Ouch!"

"Why do you get drunk at the premiere parties? I don't see you drink that much at other times. It's not like you have an alcohol problem."

"Those people make me nervous." He glanced down at his hands.

"Why?" Grace brushed her hair.

"They're professionals, experienced, famous. And I'm new, real new."

"They're just people."

"Not to me."

"Living with Cara, I'm used to them. They don't scare me."

"But at first?"

"Yeah, okay. Maybe at first."

"That's where I am. By the way. Thanks for stopping me before I got plastered."

"No problem."

"Saved me for something much better." He shot her a sexy grin as he moved his fingers over hers.

When they finished eating, Jake took her in his arms for a hug. "Why don't you get dressed while I clean up in here."

Gracie stared at him, a slow smile crept across her face. "A man who does dishes, willingly? I'm yours!" He laughed.

Grace disappeared into her bathroom and turned on the shower. Her body hummed with satisfaction, all tension gone. She sang her favorite song, "Summer Rain," in the shower. After toweling off, she threw on jeans and a sexy, dark pink T-shirt with a low-cut, ruffled neckline.

When she got back to the kitchen, Jake was wiping down the counter. "Fabulous job!"

"My sisters trained me well." His gaze wandered over her body. "You look great."

"Now for the picnic." She opened the refrigerator, then the freezer, then the cabinets.

"Hmm, it's been a while…not too much here. How about PB&J?"

"My fave, how did you know?" He came up behind her and kissed her neck.

Within half an hour, a small picnic basket had been loaded into the car, and they were heading down Mulholland Drive toward the beach. Grace drove the red, two-seater Mercedes down the familiar streets, keeping under the speed limit so Jake could soak up the scenery.

"This is some car. Love to get under the hood."

"Geez, first you want to get under my hood, now Nellie's hood. You do get around."

"Nellie? You've named the car?"

"Yup."

"Getting under your hood. Haven't heard that expression before."

"Just made it up."

"Of course, you're a writer." She shot a smile at him before turning her gaze back to the road.

Jake leaned back and rested his hand on her thigh. "Does it bother you if I do that?"

"Hell yeah, but I love it." He laughed.

They arrived at the beach by two o'clock and tore into the lunch. After eating, Jake lay down on the blanket with his hands linked behind his head. Grace cozied up to him, cuddling into his side. He wrapped an arm around her. "Life out here is nice."

"No snow."

"Sure beats the ass-freezing winters in Willow Falls."

She sat up and looked at him. "Ass-freezing?"

"Guess we can't all be writers," he chuckled.

"I like it here, too. Need to be here if I'm ever going to sell a script."

"That's tough. Probably harder than finding work acting."

"Maybe it's a tie."

He leaned over and kissed her. "You look beautiful in the sun." He held her face between his hands as he deepened the kiss. With her eyes closed, Grace could sense him moving closer, sliding on top of her. The pressure of his chest against hers lit her fire. She raised her legs, resting her feet flat on the blanket, giving him the opportunity to position himself between them, which he did. His hand covered her breast.

While the beach was almost empty, there were a few people around. *Thank God we're dressed, or he'd be inside me right now.* As his tongue tangled with hers, Grace's chest rose and fell in uneven breaths. She raised her hips slightly to meet his, causing him to moan. He lifted his head to stare into her eyes. His erection nudged her through their jeans. The heat of his stare made her want him.

"We'd better go," he said in a hoarse voice as he pushed up on his hands.

Damn! What were you going to do, strip and do him on the beach? Don't think so.

"Right. Go." She waited until he'd abandoned his position before she straightened her T-shirt and brushed her locks.

"Can't keep my hands off you," he muttered, gathering up the trash from lunch.

Gracie packed up the leftover food and put the top back on the thermos of lemonade. *Can't keep my hands off him, either.* Within fifteen minutes, they were back in the car heading to Cara's house. Grace let Jake drive. It was obvious he was enjoying it, as he commented on several aspects of the vehicle with admiration. He took her hand and rested it on his thigh while she sat back and let the wind play with her hair.

A deep feeling of contentment washed over her. Being with Jake instilled a sense of security in Grace. It was a new sensation for her, being loved by a man and comfortable with him at the same time. In the past, the guys she had been most at ease with turned out to be only friends. While the men who became lovers, getting close to her heart, made her nervous. No worries about her hair or makeup being perfect when she was with Jake.

Although she didn't understand much of what he was raving about, she enjoyed listening to him talk about cars. *Small town Jake, not movie star Jake. Talking about his hobby.*

She trained her gaze on him, and he met her eyes from time to time during a straight stretch of road. He threw her a lopsided grin, his eyes shaded by attractive sunglasses. His lips were perfect, stretched into a dazzling smile. *So kissable. How did I get this lucky?* Grace turned off her mind and let her senses take over. Happiness seeped into her heart as the sun beat down but the cool breeze kept her comfortable. *I could keep driving with him forever.*

They returned home in the late afternoon. After they put everything away, Jake took her by the elbow and sat her down next to him on the sofa in the den, facing the pool. "I'd like to take you out to the fanciest dinner…the best restaurant in town."

"Not dress-up, though, right?"

"Prefer not to dress up, but I will."

"Okay. Mojave on Rodeo Drive."

"Fine. Do we need a reservation?"

"Of course, and probably a pledge of our firstborn. It's pricey, very pricey."

"Nothing's too expensive for my girl."

Grace sidled up to him.

"Am I your girl?"

He slung his arm around her and drew her in for a hug. "Damn right you are." Jake found the number via his phone and stepped away to make the call. He chatted with a person at the restaurant for a bit before rejoining Grace. "Seems Movie Maven helped us out," he chuckled.

Her heart stopped. Her hands grew cold, and her mouth dried out. "Oh? How so?" she squeaked.

"Woman on the phone at the restaurant hadn't heard of me until she read the lousy review. She was sympathetic…and recognized my name. Without that hatchet job, we might not have our confirmed reservation at the exclusive Mojave restaurant!" He grabbed Grace and danced her around the room.

She blew out the breath she had been holding.

"Your hands are like ice," he said, draping his sweatshirt around her shoulders.

She avoided his gaze.

"Reservation's for eight. Let's practice our dance. Do you have any music?"

"For a waltz or samba?" She went to the cabinet that housed their CD collection.

"Waltz now, samba after dinner." He started moving without her.

"Why?"

"Samba warms you up for dancing between the sheets," he said, doing a turn.

"Always in the bedroom…" She shook her head. "We only have a couple of weeks left before the dance contest."

"We'll be ready."

"You're pretty confident."

He pulled her toward him, taking her hand and placing his other one on her waist. The music began. "Yep. We're meant to be."

Gracie raised her eyebrows before being carried away by the collection of Strauss waltzes and his strong arms leading her around the room in an almost perfect Viennese Waltz.

* * * *

It seemed all eyes turned to look at them when they entered Mojave. Grace wore a long, gauzy white skirt with a white cotton piqué vest, showing plenty of cleavage. Silver sandals brought her closer to Jake's height, but he still had several inches on her. He wore a blue striped sports shirt, navy sports jacket, and khaki pants.

The head waiter sat them at a cozy table in the corner. Jake slid in next to her. The bass and guitar players struck up a tune as the server took their drink order.

The soft desert colors of sandy beige, pink, and light turquoise gave the restaurant a Southwest feel. The menu followed with delicacies such as lobster enchiladas and filet mignon tacos. Two frozen strawberry margaritas arrived quickly.

"No designated driver?" she asked, taking a sip of her drink.

"I'm only going to have one. I should be okay."

"Trying to get me drunk?" She cocked an eyebrow at him.

"Should I be? Seems as if the lady's willing without alcohol."

"Don't be overconfident."

"Thought you could drink what you wanted and leave the driving to me. But if I need to get you drunk to get you into bed tonight..." he snickered.

She put her hand on his arm. "Don't think that's necessary," she whispered, right before she leaned over and kissed him, almost missing the flash of light. When she opened her eyes, a reporter took two more pictures before disappearing to a table in the back.

"Damn! No privacy. Even in a place like this," she said.

"I don't care if they publish pictures of us together. Do you?" He sipped his drink. "In fact, I'm proud to be seen with you. You're the best looking woman in this place. Probably the smartest, too."

Grace was stunned into silence by his adoration. She hid behind her drink while she gathered her thoughts.

"Don't you get it?" he whispered.

She cocked her head slightly.

"I love you." He laced his fingers with hers. "And I want everyone to know it."

"Is this your first time...feeling like this?" she asked.

"Nope. Second. But this one is much better than the first."

"My first, actually."

He raised his eyebrows. "Never been in love before?"

"In like, in lust...but never love."

His face glowed as a big smile stretched his lips. "I'm honored." He kissed her hand and another flash went off.

In a moment, the head waiter came over. "I apologize. I didn't know we had a reporter in here. He's been escorted out. I hope you're not upset."

"We're fine. No problem," Jake said. The man bowed slightly, the worried look vanished from his face, and he left. Romance was on the menu. Jake insisted they order some of the most expensive items. They shared lobster enchiladas, feeding each other little bites. Jake scooped up guacamole, prepared at their table, on a chip and deposited it into Grace's mouth, and then she returned the favor.

They snuggled close in the booth and whispered. Grace giggled a few times at Jake's funny stories about growing up in a small town. After one drink, she was euphoric. Certain it had nothing to do with alcohol but Jake's charm instead, Gracie glowed, a smile lighting up her face.

As they tucked into their desserts, a chocolate lava cake and a crème caramel, a tingle shot up Grace's spine in anticipation of the events yet to come. Jake raked his thumb across her cheek and kissed her. "Hmm, love the taste of chocolate from your lips." His eyes glowed with desire and warmth rose inside her with each touch.

If I'm dreaming, don't wake me up. She sighed.

"Tired? Not too tired...are you?" A frown furrowed his brow.

"Just happy. The...ah...uh...dessert waiting for us at home'll be..."

"Exciting," he finished for her.

"Exactly."

Jake beckoned for the check and quickly pulled out his credit card. His hand shook slightly, and Grace hid a smile at spying his nervous anticipation.

"Thank you for the great meal." Grace kissed him before they stood to leave.

He blushed and closed his fingers around hers. The valet brought the car around and opened the door for Grace. The ride home was comfortably quiet. Back at Cara's place, Jake turned up the music and they practiced their samba for an hour. Grinding their hips together and having Jake's arms around her while they danced turned her on. Heat began in her lower body and spread north until she could feel it in her neck and cheeks.

"You're flushed, want to take a break?" he asked.

Grace pulled him to her and reached up to kiss him. She eased his neck down and deepened the kiss. Pressing her hips against his, letting her passion go wild, she heard him make a deep sound in his throat as he responded. He gripped her bottom, squeezing it as his hips pushed forward. She could feel his growing erection, which simply made her hotter.

Tangled together in desire, grunts and moans the only sounds in the room, Grace's control slipped away. Jake picked her up and carried her into the bedroom. With hands shaking slightly, he unbuttoned her vest, freeing her breasts.

"No bra?" he breathed, cupping her bare flesh. "Panties?"

She nodded.

"Too bad," he said.

She reached underneath and slipped the panties down, kicking them away. "Not anymore."

Fire flickered in his eyes as he pulled her skirt to the floor and gave a low whistle. Grace unbuttoned his shirt and pushed it off his shoulders while he stepped out of his jeans. He pulled the bedcovers down and gestured for her to get in first. He followed, sliding up against her, capturing her mouth.

Passion like she had never known before coursed through her veins. She was burning up and only Jake Matthews could release her from the heat. Gripping her tightly, he ravished her with his mouth. Grace's hands traveled over his back and chest, her legs wound around his waist as the hungry pair unleashed their need.

"Take me, take me, oh God, take me," she moaned. Jake covered himself and entered her hard. She flinched.

"Did I hurt you?" He raised his eyes, seeking hers.

She shook her head. "Don't stop, oh, Jake…don't stop!" Their heat became five-alarm desire within minutes. Her face buried in his neck, she tasted his flavor mixed with a slight saltiness. She smelled the scent of freshly washed hair. Jake pulled her leg up, bending her knee and pushing in to the hilt. His hips stroked in an ever-increasing rhythm, the movement as fluid as waves in the ocean. In and out, pulling back then filling her again, creating friction and sending her senses into overdrive. She lost control, crying out his name. Her hips undulated as sweet release flooded her body.

Bending, Jake kissed and licked down to her chest then moaned loudly. Several hard thrusts and two sated, sweaty, slippery bodies came together in a fierce clinch. Panting, Jake raised his head to plant a soft kiss on Grace's lips. She combed his hair back from his forehead with her fingers.

"Awesome," he whispered.

"Amazing," she returned.

They lay gazing at each other for a while before Jake rolled off her. He glanced at the clock. "Back to reality tomorrow," he whispered.

"Don't remind me." Grace pulled the covers up over them. He switched out the light. Moonlight brightened the room a bit. She snuggled up to him. "Hold me?"

Jake positioned her on his right side, her head on his shoulder with his arm holding her firmly against him. Grace curled into him and sighed. *I feel so safe with him. In his arms nothing bad can ever happen. Movie Maven and Tiffany Cowles don't exist. It's just us. For one more night, anyway.* Contentment washed over her, bringing a smile to her lips.

"I love you so much, Gracie." He stroked her hair.

"You've changed my life, Jake."

"I don't want us to go back to the old way in New York."

"What do you mean?" She sat up and turned to him.

"Live with me."

"What?" She pulled the sheet over her chest.

"Move in with me. Then we can be together every night." He tugged the covering down to reveal her breasts kissed by the glow of the moon.

"That's a big step."

"I know."

"You sure?"

He nodded.

"Let me think about it."

"Think about this," he said, circling her peak with his finger then lowering his mouth to cover it. He raised his head and repeated softly, "every night."

"You twisted my arm."

"You will?" She nodded as he yanked her to his chest for a hug. Jake pulled the blanket over them and closed his eyes. "A dream come true," he muttered.

Gracie cuddled into him. *Safe…with Jake.* She sighed as sleep claimed her.

Chapter Eight

The next morning was like a Keystone Kops comedy. Grace and Jake forgot to set the alarm clock, so they overslept. They raced around the house packing their suitcases and cleaning up, making the place ready to sit idle for a few weeks or longer. Jake's pulse was racing. He hated to be late for anything but especially flights.

Their taxi for the airport arrived. Jake took the luggage to the car while Grace grabbed his shirt, hers, and their heavy jackets. She was buttoning her blouse when the cab pulled out of the driveway.

"Whew! I can't believe we made it," Grace said, relaxing.

"We're not there yet." He shot her a worried glance. She threaded her fingers through his.

"Everything'll be fine. We'll be there in plenty of time for Tuesday's performance."

Jake leaned back, draped his arm around her and smiled. "Probably right." When they were in the air, the steward came by with champagne, and they each took a glass. Jake cleared his throat. *Never lived with a girl before. Is it like living with my sisters only adding sex? Ew, that's disgusting.* He made a face.

"What's wrong?" Grace gazed at him.

"This'll be my first time living with a girl. Have you lived with a guy?"

She shook her head.

"Hmm. Neither one of us knows what to do."

"I'd say after these two days we both know *exactly* what to do," she snickered. The flight attendant didn't hide a smile as he walked by while Grace was speaking.

Heat traveled to Jake's face. "That's not what I mean. Yeah, we know all about that, but…"

"What's to know?"

"I mean habits. Idiosyncrasies. Stuff that can make us fight. Maybe we need…"

"Oh, no! The dreaded *rules*!" She said, covering her mouth in mock horror.

"Yeah. Rules."

"Maybe you're right. We should have some rules."

"What bugs you the most about living with roommates?"

"First–the toilet seat."

"I'm way ahead of you. I have sisters, remember? They already trained me."

"Are you neat?" She opened a package of pretzels and offered them to Jake.

"Yeah, kinda."

"Uh oh."

"You're not?" He clasped her hand in his.

"Not really. Sorta messy."

"How messy?"

"Sometimes I leave my clothes lying around the bedroom."

"Your bedroom looked fine to me. More than fine," he shot her a wicked grin.

She slapped him playfully on the shoulder. "I hadn't been there in weeks."

"I guess you'll have to walk around naked in the apartment. Then we won't have clothes everywhere…and I'll have a ton of eye candy," he chuckled.

She laughed. "We'll work it out." Jake slid his finger down her cheek. "How long will it take you to pack up?"

"Crap! I have to tell Cara." She frowned.

"What's the big deal? You're only moving a few blocks away." *If you really love me, you'll move in tonight.*

"I know that. You know that. But Cara's used to my being around twenty-four/seven."

"She'll adjust." *Come on, Gracie. Show me you love me.*

"You really want me to do this, don't you?" She stared into his eyes.

"I really do…like tonight." He leaned in and kissed her.

"Tonight?" She chewed her lip.

"Why not?" *If we wait, you'll get cold feet.*

"I have to break it to Cara, gently."

"Come on. She's got her own life. Now you'll have yours. I want you in my bed tonight. I've gotten used to having you there. I sleep better with you."

"Used to me? It's been two nights." She cocked an eyebrow at him.

"I adjust quickly. Come on, Gracie. Be with me." His pleading tone seemed to melt her resolve. *You know you want me...don't you?*

"Well..."

"We'll go right to Cara's from the airport. You'll pack up and then off to my place."

"You mean 'our' place?"

He laughed. "Yeah. Our place."

A wide grin spread over her face and a mischievous gleam lit up her eyes. "Okay!"

Jake thought his heart would burst. *She really loves me.* "Baby, I won't let you down," he whispered. "While you're packing, I'll make a set of keys for you."

The steward came by and took their order for food. Grace snuggled back into her seat.

"Sleep, honey. I've got work to do." He pulled an envelope out of his carry-on bag.

"Work?" Her question was lazy as she began to drift off.

"Gotta finish your play." She smiled as her eyes closed all the way and rested her head against him. Jake switched on the tiny overhead light and proceeded to read.

* * * *

The rest of the flight was uneventful. Excitement bubbled up in the pit of Gracie's stomach. *It's almost like a marriage proposal.* Jake's insistence on her moving into his place thrilled her to her bones. Love swelled her heart and happiness lightened her step.

Until she faced her sister.

"You're moving in with Jake? Tonight?" Cara sank down on the sofa, her face pale.

"He wants me there, and there's no reason to wait." Grace tapped her foot nervously on the hardwood floor.

"But…but you've always been there for me."

"I'll still be there for you…only a few blocks away."

Cara turned moist eyes to her sister. Alarm constricted Gracie's chest. *Damn! She's going to cry! Cara, don't. I can't take it.* "It's just an adjustment, and now that you have Grant and Sarah, you'll be too busy to miss me." She held her breath.

"Too busy? Never. We're a team. Have been for a long time. Gracie…Pookie…" Cara bit her lip. Grace sat down on the sofa and draped her arm around her sister.

"Hey, sis. It's okay. I love you a ton, you know that."

"I know, but…"

"This had to happen sooner or later."

"I'm happy for you and all, but…I feel…alone, abandoned."

"As long as I'm alive, you'll never be alone. Hey, you picked him for me, remember?"

Cara nodded, a small smile on her lips.

"Come on. Let's try it and see." Grace patted Cara on the back.

Cara stood up, blinking rapidly. But she wasn't able to stem the tide, and tears cascaded down her cheeks. Grant walked into the room and stopped in his tracks. "What the…? What happened?"

"Pookie's leaving," Cara wailed.

"Leaving?" Grant turned to look at Gracie.

"I'm moving in with Jake. Tonight." She looked at her watch. "He'll be back any minute."

"Moving in with Jake?" Grant smiled. "I know a woman in love when I see one." After taking the handkerchief Grant offered, Cara nodded.

"What's that about?" Grace asked him.

"Nothing, just a discussion with your sister. She said you weren't in love, and I said you were."

"Was I that obvious?"

"Only to the trained male eye," he chuckled. The buzzer sounded, and Cara jumped. Grace told Stokes to admit Jake and waited for him by the door.

Cara wiped her eyes and when Jake appeared she smiled. "Well, Jake, taking my girl away, huh?"

Jake shot a wary look at Grace. "Is that a problem?"

"It's fine. I have to get used to her having her own life." Cara ran her hand through Grace's locks.

Jake blew out a breath. "Good. Scared me for a minute there. Are you ready, Gracie?"

Grace hugged her sister, who wouldn't let go right away, then Grant. Jake shook hands with Grant and pecked Cara on the cheek. He picked up Grace's two suitcases and headed for the door. Grace opened it for him and turned to look one last time at her sister, who stood sniffling in the hallway. Grant wound his arm around her shoulders, and she leaned back into him. *She has Grant. She'll be all right.*

Grace gave a quick wave before she closed the door behind her. A tingle of excitement mixed with fear ran up her spine. Jake stopped and put the luggage down. He peered at her. "You all right?"

She nodded, the lump in her throat preventing her from speaking.

"That's my girl." He cupped her chin and kissed her before the elevator arrived.

Grace moved up against him, snaking her arms around his waist. *I hope I'm doing the right thing.*

"I love you, Gracie," he whispered. She grinned as she leaned into his chest.

Jake hauled the bags up the three flights to his place. Grace put on the kettle for tea while he cleared out some drawers. She looked around her new home. *This is mine now, too, right? Can I redecorate, move a few things around?* She rearranged the silverware in the drawer in the kitchen. Then she moved throw pillows from chair to sofa and from sofa to chair.

"Looks much better that way," he said, eyeing the small table now pushed against the wall. "Gives us more room."

She was surprised Jake noticed the shuffling she'd done. "You don't mind if I move a few things around?"

"This is your home now, too." He smiled and pulled her into his arms.

Grace's eyes watered. *My home, too.* She sighed and snuggled into him, grinning like the Cheshire Cat.

Life got crazy busy for Grace. Cara seemed to be more needy now that Gracie was living with Jake. She did everything she could to make her big sister's days easier. Then there was dancing. She and Jake practiced at home, at the dance studio, and even backstage before the play started. She barely had time to breathe.

During one performance, she stole into Cara's dressing room and set up her laptop. There she wrote a review of *Driving Force,* Jake's new movie. She raved about the plot, the direction, but most of all about his performance. *This should make up for the first Movie Maven review.*

> *Jake Matthews has come into his own as an actor. His performance in Driving Force is a tour de force. He captures the character perfectly, making us feel both fear of him and sympathy for him at the same time. His charisma onscreen draws you right in and keeps you there. You can't take your eyes off him. Well done, Mr. Matthews. You're the new hot actor to watch.*

She hit send, and the glowing review was on its way to Tiffany Cowles. Grace heaved a sigh of relief and closed the computer. *Need to keep this private.* She took a bottle of water from the fridge and returned to her favorite chair in the wings to watch the show. *The three of them are so good. Wish I could act.*

After the last curtain call, Jake rushed backstage. "Did you see what happened with that damn chair? I told them about that." Grace put her finger on his lips. "Let me take care of Cara, and then I want to hear all about it."

"Weren't you there? Didn't you see it?"

Grace's heart stopped.

"Where were you?"

"I…uh…I had to catch up on some email."

He arched an eyebrow. "Oh? Carrying on with another man on the Internet while I was on stage?" His tone was light, but the look in his eyes was serious.

"Of course not!"

"Sorry…I'm just a bit…never mind." He waved at her. "Take care of Cara."

When she finished with her sister, she joined Jake for the short walk a few blocks home. "What was that jealousy about? A man on the Internet?"

Jake blushed and dropped his gaze to the sidewalk.

"Come on. Give. We're living together, tell me!" She shook his shoulder.

"Remember I said you weren't the first for me?"

She nodded.

"The first girl I loved cheated on me. Traci."

"Oh my God! She broke your heart?" Gracie asked, clutching her jacket over the left side of her chest.

"Yeah. She was seeing another guy on the side. Dumped me for him because I was an unemployed actor, and he was headed for Wall Street. Bitch."

"Terrible. Awful. I'm so sorry. I'd never do that." She slipped her hand into his.

"I couldn't hack it if you did."

"Never." She shook her head for emphasis. *Who cheats on a guy like this? Doesn't get better than Jake.* They walked on in silence for a few moments until Grace stopped. *It's now or never. Tell him how you feel.*

"I love you. I've never said that to another guy. You mean…everything to me." Being emotionally naked in front of him caused her to shiver. Jake wrapped his arms around her, hugging her tightly.

They stopped at their favorite pizza place and picked up a pie to go. In Jake's tiny studio, they ate, made love and showered together. Jake was exhausted as always after a show, so he fell asleep right away, but Grace lay awake. She stared out the window at the full moon and smiled. *I am the luckiest girl in the world.*

He rolled over, tossing his arm carelessly over her waist and murmured a few unintelligible words. Grace wiggled back into him, sighing at the feel of his warmth against her. With a full heart, she closed her eyes and fell into a deep, dreamless sleep.

* * * *

The next morning, Grace rolled over and snuggled up to Jake. The alarm went off, and the couple groaned as he reached for the clock. "Damn clock. Hell, it's only nine." He rolled over.

Grace threw the covers off. "Time to get up. We have to practice. Dorrie's expecting us."

"Do we have to?" Jake shoved the pillow over his head.

"We have to." Grace tugged the bedclothes down. Jake covered his face with his hands before grabbing the sheet. The two naked lovers tussled in a game of tug of war, laughing and giggling. Jake won as he yanked all the coverings completely off the bed and rolled over on top of Grace.

He placed a hard kiss on her mouth. "I win! Winner gets to choose next activity."

"Like I don't know what you'll pick?" She cocked an eyebrow at him.

"If you guessed making love, you'd be right." By ten thirty, they were entering the empty dance studio. Dorrie greeted them with a frown. "Hey, I expected you guys an hour ago." She rested her hand on her hip. Grace lowered her gaze as she sensed heat in her cheeks.

"Oh. I get it. Something else was more...*pressing*?" She giggled. Grace glanced at Jake, whose face was red as a beet.

"Start the music!" She raced over to the player and put in their Strauss CD.

"Waltz? I thought you'd mastered that. How's the samba coming?" Dorrie turned her attention back to the dance.

Jake pulled Grace into position before he answered, "We've nailed samba. Now, waltz." He twirled Gracie around the room in perfect sync to the music. After an hour, they took a break.

"You two are naturals. You're such perfect partners, I'd swear you're sleeping together," she chuckled. Grace checked her phone and found seven messages from Tiffany Cowles. Excusing herself, Grace fled to the ladies room to view the texts. Leaning against the cool white tile wall, she cringed as each one got angrier and more hostile than the one before.

A nice review? What are you thinking?

This stinks. It's so sweet it's attracting ants.

I'm not publishing this crap. You can do better.

If you don't stop sending this garbage, there will be consequences.

My eyes hurt from all the sweet crap in your review.

This is unprofessional. I'm not publishing it.

Lauding your boyfriend's performance isn't very professional. Stop this nonsense and send me what I want. How would your BF feel if he found out who Movie Maven really is?

At the last message, Grace gave out a little gasp. *She wouldn't, would she?*

"What's the matter?" Dorrie stood in the doorway, looking concerned.

"Nothing, nothing." Grace quickly closed her phone.

"Then finish up. I've got a class coming in fifteen minutes." Gracie nodded and returned to Jake. But her pulse was beating wildly, and her palms were sweating. She wiped her hands on her leotard before clasping Jake's.

"Are you okay? You look pale."

"I'm fine. Let's go. Only fifteen minutes then we have to leave." Dorrie flipped on the music, and the pair whirled around the dance floor, executing the perfect Viennese Waltz. Grace found it hard to focus at first as fear coursed through her veins. *Tiffany would never do that. She's bluffing.* Certain in her belief that Tiffany Cowles had a heart, Grace relaxed, focusing her attention on Jake, their dance steps, and the beat.

The day passed quickly. Again that evening during the performance, Grace slipped into Cara's dressing room and posted her glowing review of *Driving Force* on Movie Maven's blog. Though she only managed a post a week there, she had a big following.

A grin stole across her face as she exercised her own power to post this rave in spite of Tiffany. *She doesn't own me. Fine. Don't publish it. I'll publish it myself. Not as many people will see it, but enough.* Checking her watch, she scurried back to her place in the wings. *Must get back before Jake misses me.*

She slid into her seat a few seconds before Jake's exit. His warm smile was her reward for being quick. "Good house tonight. Real good," he muttered to her as he squeezed her shoulder and turned, waiting for his cue to return to the stage.

On their way home from the theater, they decided to stop at Grant's favorite Italian restaurant, *Trieste,* for pasta. After a glass of wine, Jake took Grace's hand. "I passed your script on to Quinn. I hope you don't mind."

"You did? Why?"

"Because I thought it was great. Really good. His wife is a close friend of Max Webster. Anyway, wanted to get his opinion."

"The show's producer? Quinn's too busy to read it…"

"He said he'd start it on Monday."

"Oh. God. Hope he likes it." She put her head in her hands.

"He will. You're good." The waiter brought a platter of rigatoni with a tomato sauce and big chunks of sausage and placed it between them. They dug into the food like they hadn't eaten in years. Grace concentrated on Jake's new stories about Willow Falls and pushed the nagging fear that Tiffany would act on her threat out of her mind. *I deserve to enjoy my time with Jake. Not to worry all the time.*

Jake's phone rang. "It's Quinn. Better take it." He put down his fork. After a brief conversation he hung up, smiling.

"What?" She asked, taking another forkful from the platter.

"Seems as if I finally did something right."

"And what would that be?"

"*Driving Force.* The Movie Maven gave it a rave review. Quinn read her comments about me. Maybe you'd better look out. I could love a woman who said those things." He chuckled.

You already do. Grace leaned over and kissed him. "I'm glad you got a good review."

"My ego could use a little stroking after the beating I took from her."

"I'd love to read it. Like to know my competition," she joked.

"No competition for you, baby," he whispered and returned her kiss.

* * * *

Grace loved Monday the most because it was Jake's day off. They lingered in bed—no rehearsal, no show. The day was spent being together, shopping, exploring the museum, and trying out new restaurants. Jake was generous, taking her to expensive shops and tony eateries, always picking up the tab.

She was embarrassed when he spent money on her, but he seemed to enjoy it. Life resembled her version of a fairytale. While she expected Cara to end up with the perfect marriage and an adoring husband, she never thought she'd have a relationship that could compare.

Their couple-dom did not go unnoticed. Once Tiffany Cowles was on their trail, so was every other paparazzi in town. They were photographed dining out, shopping, strolling down Central Park West to Cara's and almost every place else, including leaving Dorrie's dance studio.

While Jake was accustomed to photographers and understood how important publicity was for his career, shy Gracie had yet to adjust. Red spots appeared in front of her eyes for hours after flashes went off in her face. She didn't know how to anticipate the photos and was often caught in an unflattering pose or expression.

Jake laughed about her naiveté and tried to smooth her ruffled feathers, so she determined to become as adept at he was at handling unexpected photo-ops. They bought the newspapers and had a contest to see who could find their pictures first in each one.

On this Saturday evening after the show, as they were leaving their building to grab a Sunday Times newspaper, they were surprised by four photographers all from different papers. Jake took Grace's hand and smiled at the cameras.

"Smile, Gracie," he hissed between clenched teeth. Before she could change her expression, Mark from *Celebs 'R Us* stepped forward, turned to her and, in a loud voice, said, "Hey, look. It's the Movie Maven!"

"Where?" Jake asked, turning his head to the left then back again.

Grace froze for a second. Ice surrounded her heart. She tightened her grip on Jake's hand and started to run. "Psst, Jake, this way," she whispered.

"Don't run from me, Movie Maven. Let me get a nice shot of you and your boyfriend...the one you slammed in my paper, *Celebs 'R Us?*" He took a picture, the flash temporarily blinding Grace.

Jake halted in his tracks. He pulled Grace to him. "You're not? You can't be? Please tell me he's joking!" The pleading look in Jake's eyes tore out her heart. She had no breath for an answer.

"Jake Matthews meet Grace Brewster, A.K.A. the Movie Maven," the reporter said.

"No, no, it can't be. Say it isn't true, Gracie," Jake begged her as he gripped her arms hard. Grace's pulse beat wildly. Her mouth went dry as she searched her mind for a way out. The photographer stood by, waiting to take his next photo.

"Do you mind? I'd like to have a private conversation with my girl," Jake snapped.

"Hey, this is a public street, buddy. If you want private, go somewhere else." Jake made a fist and took a threatening step toward the photographer, who raised his hands. "Hey, I just take pictures. It's her you want to sock."

Grace pulled on his arm. Pain squeezed her heart. She couldn't let Jake get into a fist fight over her. "Stop, Jake. Please. I can explain," she said in a quiet voice. The look of shock on his face crushed her courage. Mark snapped several photos while the couple froze in their positions. Jakes eyes searched hers. She blinked back tears and took a shaky breath. "I..."

"You've been the Movie Maven all this time?"

She nodded once. "But I can explain."

He continued as if he hadn't heard her, "And you didn't tell me?" The flashes kept flashing. Jake finally turned to the crowd and chased them halfway down the block. When he returned, fury shot from his eyes, his expression stormy.

"Grace Brewster, how could you?" He came at her aggressively, his voice seething, his anger barely controlled.

She backed away in fear, her eyes wide. "Please...it was meant for Gunther..."

"I'm not talking about what you wrote…but you didn't tell me. Kept this secret…a damn big secret…from me."

"I thought you'd be upset…and see, I was right." He grabbed her arms and gripped her tight. "Ow, you're hurting me." The fury on his face calmed for a second as he loosened his grip slightly.

"We're living together…almost engaged, and you don't tell me something this big? How can I trust you? What else are you keeping from me? Maybe a marriage or two? Do you have any *other* secret identities?"

She shook her head vigorously. "No secrets, no marriages, no identities."

"How can I believe you?"

"You can, Jake, I didn't mean to hurt you, I…"

"A scathing review aimed right at me, and you don't tell me you wrote it. You didn't mean to hurt me? You expect me to believe that?"

"I do, I do. Please." Tears could no longer be controlled as she watched his expression turn from white-hot rage to ice.

"I think you'd better stay at Cara's tonight."

"Won't you let me explain?"

"There's nothing to explain. You wanted to hurt Gunther and me. And you did. And you lied to me…"

"I didn't lie. I never said I wasn't…"

"Don't play word games with me, Grace. You lied by not coming clean. Now I can't trust you. And what a vengeful thing to do over…I don't know. I don't know you. Thought I did, thought you were a kind, caring, sweet woman…but I was wrong."

Jake dropped his hands and shoved them in the pockets of his pants. As he backed away from her, she saw the cold expression on his face melt away only to be replaced by a look of hurt. "I trusted you. You betrayed that trust."

Grace wiped her tears. "Please give me a chance."

He shook his head slowly before turning his back on her and walking toward his apartment. Grace stood alone on the dark street, sobs wracking her body. She lifted a shaking arm to flag down a taxi on Broadway. Fumbling in her purse, she finally located a clean tissue. As she was wiping her face, a cab stopped. She got in and gave Cara's address.

As the car sped up Broadway, Grace turned to look for Jake. They passed him, allowing Grace one last glimpse of him for the night. Her heart shattered. *I had it all, my own fairytale, and I wrecked it.*

Chapter Nine

She sat back in the cab, staring with unseeing eyes out the window. The lights of New York at night blurred into one long, yellow brilliance splitting the darkness as the taxi shot up the avenue. Emotional pain mixed with physical pain until she ached all over. Clutching her purse to her bosom as if it were a lover, she tried to keep her breathing steady to calm herself. *Wait until you get to Cara's. Just wait.*

The vehicle screeched to a halt in front of The Stanford, Rex, the doorman, greeted her. Grace's hearing had shut down, but she saw his lips move, so she nodded to him. After stuffing a small wad of bills into the tiny payment compartment, she slid across the seat. Later she wouldn't remember the ride home, paying the driver, or even coming upstairs.

Her hand shook as she aimed the key in the right direction, but didn't connect. Finally able to steady one with her other, she jammed the key in the lock and turned. Grant was right behind the door when she opened it. "Gracie, it's you. I thought someone was trying to break in."

Grace looked up at him and tears began to form again, but words wouldn't come. Grant stepped back to let her in the house. "Grant! Who's at the door?" Cara called from the living room.

"It's Gracie." Grace stood frozen, watching Cara enter the hall. At the sight of her sister, Grace's defenses fell away. She let out a cry as the floodgates opened up, burying her face in her hands. Cara's arms were around her in a heartbeat.

"Pookie! Darling, what's wrong? What is it? Did something happen to Jake? Talk to me?"

Grace couldn't hear what her sister was saying, because she had lost control. Sobbing, she began to sink to the floor. Grant grabbed her around the waist, and he and Cara slowly moved her to her small room. Once inside, they eased her down on the bed. Grace stopped to gasp for air.

Grant whipped out a handkerchief and handed it to her. She cleaned up her face and steadied her breathing.

"Take your time, Pookie." Grace gave a small smile at the endearment. "What happened?"

"Jake broke up with me."

"What? Why?"

"Tonight we met some…he found out…" She stopped to take a deep breath. "I'm the Movie Maven…and tonight, Jake found out."

Cara gasped as her hand flew to her mouth. "Gracie, you're not. Tell me you're not."

"Who's the Movie Maven?" Grant seemed confused.

"A woman who wrote horrible, scathing reviews of Gunther's movies…everybody's movies for *Celebs 'R Us,*" Cara said.

"I am, Cara. I am." Grace hung her head.

"Why?"

"Because of what Gunther did."

"But Jake?"

"Never mind. It doesn't matter. The things he did were jerky but didn't deserve that."

"Then why?"

"I was angry…furious…at Gunther, at myself. I'd been betrayed, and I wanted revenge."

"Oh, baby. If only you'd come to me…"

"What could you have done, Cara? What? Nothing!" Grace bounded off the bed. "You can't fix everything, Carol Anne. You can't. I know you want my life to be perfect…me to be perfect, but I'm not. And this time I made the biggest mistake ever. I didn't tell Jake. I should have. He trusted me. Then he finds out I have this other…persona, identity, whatever. A big secret."

Cara and Grant were silent.

"He's right, you know. He's right. I blew it, destroyed what we had."

"You told him about Gunther, why couldn't you tell him about this?" Cara asked.

"Because I was afraid…afraid he'd be mad at me for slamming him. I was pretty nasty. I knew he'd be hurt. I was afraid I'd lose him. And I was right."

"So what happened?"

Grace explained about Tiffany's threat when she'd stopped the bad reviews. Grant and Cara were sympathetic. Cara hugged her and rose to leave.

"Oh my God," Gracie moaned.

Cara turned at the door. "What?"

"Wait until Gunther finds out." She shuddered as she sank down on her bed, her head in her hands.

"Gunther Quill is not a man to trifle with, Gracie."

"Figured." Fear shot through her veins. "What do you think he'll do?"

"Let's hope he'll consider you small potatoes and do nothing," Cara said as she left the room.

Something tells me he's not a man to sit by and not retaliate when attacked. She turned out the light and buried her head under her pillow, as if she could hide from the wrath of the powerful Mr. Quill.

Unable to sleep, Grace paced, drank coffee, tried to write a note to Jake at least three times, and then paced some more. By six o'clock she was completely exhausted and fell asleep. She awoke at eleven to a silent house. Sarah was at school, Grant at work, and Cara on her way to the theater.

Matinée day! Jake will be at the theater soon, too. She showered and dressed in jeans and a sweater. By one she left the apartment, heading to Jake's. She let herself in quietly then called his name twice to make certain he wasn't home. *Matinée starts at two. He can't still be here.*

Quickly she packed her things and put her keys on the kitchen counter. She read the letter she wrote one more time.

> *You're right. I should have told you. I love you, but I understand why we can't be together anymore. I'm so sorry I wrecked everything between us. I didn't mean to.*
> *Grace*

She folded the paper, kissed it, and placed it beside the keys. She managed to get the heavy suitcases out the door and into a taxi. With a deep sigh, she watched Jake's building disappear as the cab rode north.

Unpacking was the hardest thing she'd ever done. With every garment she placed in the bureau or closet, she envisioned how happy she had been with Jake. Only a week of living with him, but night after night being together at the theater, watching him perform, making love with him, dancing, eating pizza, telling jokes…there were so many things about their time together she loved and nothing she hated.

Hanging up her lavender silk dress, she shrank back in horror. *Damn!* Her sexy outfit for dancing the samba hung there, innocently mocking her. *The dance contest is tonight!* A soft pink chiffon dress to wear for the waltz hung next to the fiery samba ensemble. *No, no, no. Not dancing tonight. No way. If I go and he doesn't show up, I'll die. I'm not going. Jake's not going to be there. He couldn't even look me in the eye, let alone dance with me.*

A new heaviness entered her heart. Something else she wanted she wouldn't have. She sank down on the bed and heaved a long sigh. Lying back, she pulled the quilt around her. Suddenly, exhaustion trumped being upset, and she fell asleep.

At three o'clock she awoke. *The show's over.* She turned off her cell phone and put on her coat, heading to *The Blue Heron* bar on Eighth Avenue. She and Jake went in there from time to time. They knew the bartender.

"Hi, Barry."

"Hey, Grace. What can I do for you?"

"How about a margarita, straight up, and some chicken fingers?"

"Coming right up." She took a table in the corner and took a swig of her drink. The alcohol was cold and soothing going down. *I need to stop the pain.* Grace sat back and watched the old reliables file in. As a writer, she enjoyed watching people and trained her quiet gaze on the men and women who chose this tavern to ice their troubles in.

She finished her margarita and ordered another. A quick glance at the clock told her it was four o'clock. *Dance contest is at eight. Gotta a lot of time to kill here.* She nibbled on the chicken fingers and listened in on conversations.

* * * *

At the theater, Jake rushed into Cara's dressing room right after the show. "Where's Grace?"

"I don't know. Home I'd guess. She was pretty upset."

Jake lowered his gaze, trying to hide his embarrassment. "I was a little harsh with her last night."

"I don't want to interfere. Please don't put me in the middle," Cara said.

"Tonight's the dance contest. She's supposed to be here."

"Did you call her?"

"Straight to voicemail."

"Damn!"

"I'm going home and see if she's there."

"Didn't you tell her to move out?"

"I only asked her to spend last night at your place."

Cara cocked an eyebrow at him. "Isn't that the same thing, Jake?"

"I don't know. Maybe. I didn't mean it to be. I'm willing to listen to her side today."

"You might not get a chance."

"Hey, wouldn't you have been pissed?"

"I suppose. Look. Leave me out. Okay? She's my sister, and you're my co-star...I'm right in the middle. Yipes! I don't really know what happened and don't want to. You two have to work it out." Cara opened her door, indicating that Jake should leave.

"Will you call me if you find her?"

"I will. I'm sure she'll be at the dance contest tonight. Not like Gracie to run out on a commitment."

"Not so sure," he said under his breath, as he headed down the hall to his room. Jake waited another hour and called Grace about five times before he headed home. After opening the door to his apartment, he called her name. No answer. Hoping a beer would calm his nerves, he went to the refrigerator. There he spied the keys and the note on the counter. *Oh, no. Gracie!* A new pain entered his heart.

Last night he had been upset. Worried that he'd rushed into his relationship with Gracie, not knowing her well enough, he'd determined to have a long talk with her before deciding what to do. Now her departure short-circuited that. *Dammit!*

He threw the note in the trash, chugged his beer and sat down with his cell phone. *Must find Grace. Need to talk.* He called Cara, then Dorrie Rogers. But Gracie wasn't on Central Park West, and she wasn't at the studio. He called Quinn, but neither he nor Susanna had seen Grace.

Now it was six o'clock, and time was getting short. He called Cara again. "Bring her costumes to the studio, please. Come half an hour early."

"Will do. Have you heard from her?"

"Not yet. You?" Jake paced.

"Nope."

"See you later."

He hung up and got his coat. *Hmm. Smuggler's Cove, The Blue Heron, Casey's Place...one by one until I find her.* He entered Smuggler's Cove and went straight to the bar.

"Have you seen Gracie, George?" The bartender shook his head. "Should I tell her you're looking for her if she shows up?"

"Nah. Never mind. I want to surprise her."

As he walked down the street, he couldn't keep his mind from going over and over what had happened between them. Guilt fought with indignation, mistrust battled with love in his heart. Instead of finding a solid answer, he only became more confused. *Is it my fault she moved out? Did I tell her to? I thought I only said I wanted to spend one night apart. Maybe she thought...I said...I don't know. Women, dammit!*

When he walked into *The Blue Heron*, Barry nodded at him then glanced over to the corner where Gracie was sitting. Jake approached her slowly. She was looking at her drink and didn't notice him.

"Is this seat taken?" Jake stood next to her.

Grace's head snapped up, and she stared at him. Her eyes filled with tears as she pushed the chair toward him with her foot. He sat down and moved closer. A waitress stopped by, but Jake waved her off.

"Hey! I wanted another drink."

"Looks like you've had enough, Grace."

She turned hostile eyes to him. "Says who?"

"I do."

"You have no right...you gave that up last night."

"What? What did I give up? I wanted to spend one night apart. Wanted to think...by myself. I didn't tell you to move out!" Jake raised his voice.

"Stop shouting at me!" A few tears spilled over and ran down her cheek.

"We're dancing tonight." He strained to control his anger and to speak in a quiet tone.

"Are we?" She turned a belligerent face toward him.

"We are. No more drinks. How many have you had already?"

"Two...I think."

"You think? How are you going to dance, drunk?"

"I'm not drunk, and I'm not going to dance."

"Really? I'm your partner, and I say you are."

"You're not my partner. You were...until last night," she said in a soft voice.

"I am. At least I'm still your dance partner."

Grace wiped her tears with her hand. "That's all you are. And now," she waved in the air, "you're not that anymore, either."

"Why are you doing this?"

"You threw me out last night, remember?"

"I didn't...throw you out. I wanted to spend one night apart. I thought we could talk today, but you disappeared."

"I hate people who push themselves on others, stay where they're not wanted..."

"You mean me?" Pain seared his chest.

"Me, stupid! Me! You told me to go away last night, and so I did. I'll never bother you again." He heard the strain in her voice.

"I don't want you to go away," he softened his tone. "Please dance with me, Gracie."

Her gaze searched his face. He took her hand, and she let him hold it for a few seconds before slipping it out of his grasp.

"Come on. We worked so hard. We're good, and Dorrie is counting on us. They sold a bunch of tickets...it's for charity. They're expecting us."

"And if I do...then what?"

"I don't know." *Tell her you still care about her. Say something!*

She gasped and more tears slid down her face.

"I was hurt. Don't know what to do." Jake looked down. *You're making it worse.*

"Do you still have feelings for me?" she croaked out.

"Do you?" he asked, stubbornly refusing to admit how much he cared for her.

"It's wrecked now. I've wrecked it."

He glanced at his watch. *Shit, it's seven!* "Would you please dance with me?"

"Okay."

"Are you sober enough?"

"Of course. Two drinks. That's all." She stood up, wobbled for a second, then giggled. Jake palmed her elbow, guiding her outside. He flagged down a taxi, and they went straight to the studio.

"Wait! My costumes…"

"Cara's bringing them."

* * * *

The next hour was a blur to Grace. Jake walked her around the block, talking to her, while he waited for Cara to show up with her costumes. The studio began to fill up, and Gracie's nerves were shot. The heaviness in her chest prevented anxiety but weighed her down. Cara arrived twenty-five minutes before show time and dragged Grace backstage. "Take off your clothes," her sister barked.

"Wish you were Jake saying that," Gracie kidded. Cara shot her sister a sharp look. "I'm not too happy with you. Disappearing like that. Scaring the hell out of me, Jake, Grant…and Dorrie almost had a heart attack! So shut up and do as you're told."

Grace undressed and followed her sister's instructions without uttering a word. *I've let everyone down. Been a baby. Time to man up.*

Cara pinned up her sister's hair for the samba, their first number. Grace slipped on her black satin heels and tiptoed out of the dressing room and into the wings. Her outfit consisted of a black lace bra corset combination over black lace stockings, and a black satin short skirt split up the side with red ruffles. Jake was there in his costume, looking more handsome than he had a right to. Her gaze traveled over his body in the tight black suit that clung in all the right places, with a dark red shirt open to the navel.

"You look amazing," she whispered.

His stare moved down her body, heating her insides. "So do you," he whispered back.

"When do we go on?"

"Two more dances."

"Should we warm up?"

"I thought we did, walking around outside."

"Oh, yeah. But I need something more…before we go on."

Jake faced her. "What?"

She glanced at the ground, nervously chewing her lip.

"What?" he repeated.

"Nothing." *A kiss would warm me up for the samba. A kiss would be wonderful…not gonna happen because you blew it.*

He got closer to her and draped his arm around her waist. Grace closed her eyes and sank into his shoulder. When the music stopped, the couple dancing received applause then left the temporary stage. Then, the next couple came on and their song was cued.

"We're next," Jake whispered. The dance seemed to take only thirty seconds and before she knew it, Grace heard Dorrie announce them.

"Grace Brewster and Jake Matthews!"

He took her hand, and they went on stage. They struck their poses and as the music began, their chemistry kicked in. The song was seductive. Jake was masterful and sexy. The sway of their hips pulled her into the number in a way it hadn't quite before. Relaxed by the alcohol, Grace bent to his commands with ease and fluidity. The sexual tension between them fairly crackled like a loose power line.

They slinked across the stage, stopping to grind their hips together, shake top to bottom and then execute the intricate steps in unison with each other and the music. The heat they generated was enough to wilt the flowers in her hair as well as stoke smoldering fires within her. She wanted him.

When the dance was over, the audience leapt to their feet, applauding. Grace and Jake bowed. Then, to each other, and Jake kissed her hand. Back stage, he hugged her.

"I've got to change!" Grace ran off to the dressing room where Cara was waiting for her. Off with the sexy samba costume and on with the filmy, chiffon dress for the Viennese Waltz.

"That was some steamy dance, Pookie," Cara said, unzipping Grace's outfit.

"You liked it?"

"It was great. You two were smokin' hot. Is it like that off stage, too?"

"Cara!"

"What?" Cara hung up the samba costume.

"Pretty nosy, aren't you?" Grace snatched the waltz costume off the chair.

"So? I'm your sister."

"You're not entitled to know everything about me." Grace wiggled into the dress.

"Says who?"

"Why don't you tell me how hot you and Grant are?"

Cara stopped. "Okay. You win." Cara zipped the back up.

"Hair?"

"Must be different. Long and loose," Cara said, brushing Grace's locks.

"It's weird having you do this for me."

"I know. I like it." Cara grinned at her little sister. "Break a leg…do you say that for a dance contest?" the actress's brow furrowed.

"Not sure. But I get it."

"Now go. Dance with the man of your dreams and forget about everything else." Cara hugged her sister and returned to her seat.

I'll try. Man of my dreams? Maybe I was just dreaming. She sighed and slipped backstage to meet Jake. Grace stood in the wings, waiting for the couple doing a Pasa Doble to finish. Jake joined her. He gave her a small smile and a nod of approval before taking her into his embrace. She loved how strong his hands were, and always warm and dry.

"Back by popular demand, doing the Viennese Waltz, Grace Brewster and Jake Matthews," Dorrie said, and then led the applause as the couple took their place on the stage. The music flowed sweetly as Grace and Jake formed a frame with their shoulders. A lightness in her step enabled her to float across the floor in Jake's arms.

As she gave herself over to the rhythm of the music, her tension and anxiety melted away. When she looked into his eyes, it became only Grace and Jake dancing together in perfect harmony. The audience, and even Dorrie, fell away for Grace as Jake whirled her around the room with subtle pressure from his fingers on her waist. *Lovely, beautiful.*

Their perfect timing and the way their bodies flowed as one told Grace they belonged together. She refused to think but simply to feel the joy coursing through her as she put herself in his capable hands.

The music ended too soon. Again they received 'bravo' cheers, tons of applause, and a standing ovation. After their bows to the audience and each other, reality came crashing down on Grace as Jake's expression became hooded. She sensed him pulling back from her and stepped aside to let him go. *Only way to hold him is to let him go.*

Emotion rose in her chest, making speech impossible. She fled to her dressing room and closed the door. With trembling hands, she fussed with the zipper until Cara arrived.

"Let's go out and celebrate, Pookie," Cara said, folding the chiffon dress while Grace slipped into her sweater and jeans. When they returned to the studio, most of the people had left. Grant, Sarah, and Dorrie were waiting.

"Ah, ladies! A fine dance, Gracie. Beautiful. Let's go to Hark's Cabin for a bite and some champagne." Grant turned from Grace to Dorrie. "Will you join us?"

"How lovely. Let me get my coat."

"Where's Jake?" Grace asked.

Grant's face turned pink and his gaze slid to the floor. "He's gone."

* * * *

Jake wasn't happy with himself for skipping out on Grace after the dance. *Left her without a word. Coward!* He was confused and needed time to think. Then he needed to talk to Grace. Maybe.

He pulled the collar of his coat up against the early spring wind as he walked down Broadway toward his building.

When? When am I going to talk to her? What am I going to say? I didn't mean to break us up, did I? Maybe I did. How would I feel if Grace had asked to take a night off from me? Probably would have been fine with it. She overreacted. Typical female.

The air was much colder than when he went to look for Grace, and his thin jacket wasn't keeping him very warm. Jake shivered as a gust of wind blew right through the fabric, chilling his arms and neck. He increased his pace. *Only two more blocks.*

When he entered his apartment, the first thing he did was put hot water in the coffeemaker. *Need something warm.* Reluctant to take off his jacket, he slumped down on the sofa and stretched out. The rooms were warm but drafty near the windows, so he stayed curled up on the convertible couch that made into a bed. By the time the coffee was ready, Jake was already asleep, clothes and all. After half an hour, the machine shut off.

At three o'clock in the morning, Jake's phone rang. He hid his head under a pillow, but the incessant ringing wouldn't stop. Cracking his eyes open, he looked at the display. *Gunther Quill. What the fuck does he want at this hour?* Jake answered.

"Jake! You're home!"

"It's three in the morning, Gunther. What do you want?"

"Oh, right, right. Three hour difference…sorry about that, old chap."

"What's up? Are you plastered?"

"Had a few. I admit it. Still…"

"What?"

"Oh, yeah. Reason I called. Found out Grace Brewster is Movie Maven."

"Yeah, so?"

"That bitch…that little bitch! She panned my movies…dumped on them royally. She probably hurt sales. Dumped on you, too, buddy."

I'm not your buddy, Gunther. "Your point is?"

"I'm getting there. Don't rush me."

"Look…I'd like to get back to sleep?"

"Oh. Yeah. Sorry. Point is, now it's payback time. Time to destroy her. I'm gonna call every producer and director I know. Gonna make sure they know her secret identity."

"Don't do that."

"I am. And you're gonna, too. Look at what she did to you!"

"Gunther…"

"She humiliated you in front of the whole movie industry…"

"Not really."

"She did. '*Most-wooden-performance-of-the-year award. I wanted to take his pulse to see if he was still alive. As a romantic lead he has the sex appeal of a slug. His performance put me to sleep.*' What more do you need to hear?"

Jake gritted his teeth, warding off the renewed sting of those words…that had already been burned on his brain, the first time he had read them. Still, he would not retaliate. As outrageous as her actions were, he had behaved very badly toward her. Maybe he deserved such a public slap in the face. "No way. Not going to do anything."

"What? You're going to let that little…little…"

"Watch it, Gunther. She's my girlfriend."

"Still? Even after this? Oh, I forgot. You're banging her, so you're going to turn the other cheek? Well, not me. If you won't help me destroy her, I'll do it by myself."

"Don't, Gunther!" Jake fairly screamed into the mouthpiece.

"She deserves it."

"You had it coming. She's a nice kid, give her a break. You owe her, anyway, after what you did."

"Owe her? I don't think so. What did I do? Sleep with a beautiful, willing young woman? Since when is that against the law?"

"Come on. We both know the truth."

"Yeah? Well, prove it. In a court of law. Until then, she'll never be able to show her face in Hollywood, after I get through with her."

"Do the decent thing, Gunther."

"Why should I? Go ahead, Jake, be a chump. Hang out with her and see how much work you get."

"Are you threatening me?"

"Just telling you the truth." With that, the line went dead.

Jake punched his fist into a pillow on the sofa. He heated up the cold coffee because he sure wasn't going back to sleep. Thank God it was Monday, his day off. *Think, think. Gotta be some way to stop him.*

Jake paced a bit, ending up at the window. New York City was quiet at that hour. An occasional drunken couple staggered down the street singing, a few taxicabs drove by, but otherwise the city was asleep. *Quinn! Quinn'll know what to do. He's got a great rep. He'll help.* Once he had an action to take, Jake calmed down. Suddenly exhausted, he stretched out on the sofa again and was asleep quickly.

Chapter Ten

When Jake arrived at Quinn's apartment, he realized he had interrupted an intimate moment. Both Quinn and his wife, Susanna, were wearing robes and had a slight flush to their faces. *Idiot! Should have called first.*

Holding up his phone, Quinn said, "Have you met this yet, Jake? It's called the cell phone."

"I'm so sorry…didn't realize…I should have called first."

"Damn right. This had better be urgent. My day off is…my time with Susie."

"Sit down, Jake. Don't mind, Quinn. He's always grumpy before nine on his day off. I'll put up some coffee. Don't say anything important until I get back."

Jake paced, too nervous to sit.

"Hey, you're making me tired, just watching…and wearing out the rug."

"Sorry. I can't sit. Gunther Quill is going to be on the move soon, and I need to do something."

"Hey! I told you not to say anything important until I got back!"

"Sorry," Jake called into the kitchen. He sat down on the sofa, got up, slumped into a chair, got up, and tried the sofa again.

"Hurry up in there, Susanna. This guy's driving me crazy out here."

Finally, she walked in carrying a tray with three mugs of coffee, milk, and sugar. "Okay, Jake. Fire away."

The story about Gunther Quill's threat to Grace spilled out rapid-fire, until he got to the part about why she did it.

"And why did Grace attack his film…and you?" Quinn cocked an eyebrow.

"I can't tell you that. She told me in confidence. It's personal. Trust me she had a good reason to lash out at him. Though, maybe this wasn't the best way to do it."

"Come on, Jake. You tell me this exciting story and leave out the best part. Revenge, what drives it? Gotta know."

"I'm sorry, Quinn, I can't."

"So what are we going to do to save Grace? Does she know he's gunning for her?" Susanna asked.

"I don't think so." Jake sat back and sipped his coffee. Knowing his friends would help brought some relief and loosened his muscles a bit.

"I'll talk to him," Quinn volunteered.

"Don't! I don't want him to trash you, too," Jake said.

"Maybe we should ask Grace…and Cara? She seems to know Gunther pretty well. Isn't she considering doing a movie with him?"

"Yeah. Good." He nodded.

"You've got to tell Grace," Susanna put in.

"Me?" His eyebrows rose.

"You're her guy, so yeah." Quinn concurred with his wife.

"Oh, no. Not sure we're still a couple."

"What happened?" Susanna asked.

Jake related a shorthand version of their fight and break-up. They were silent for a while.

"You should be spending time on singing lessons and dancing lessons, not getting wiped out by some chick. You're new to this business, Jake. Got a lot to learn."

"I didn't plan on her. Believe me."

"But it happened. And now?" Susanna prompted.

"Now? I don't know," Jake said, shaking his head, staring at the floor.

"But you want to save her."

"Yeah. Can't let Gunther take another shot at her…her writing." He jumped to his feet and began to pace.

"Loved her screenplay, by the way. Susanna passed it on to Max."

"Great! Until he hears from Gunther, that is."

"Max Webster is his own man. He won't follow Gunther."

"I hope. Still, bad publicity…"

"Call Cara. She'll know what to do." Quinn said.

"Could you call her? Invite her over? I don't want to talk to Grace right now."

"Why not?" Quinn asked.

"Don't know what to say." Jake picked at a loose thread on his shirt.

"That's cowardly, isn't it?" Susanna said, as gently as she could.

"Maybe. Until I fix this Gunther thing…"

"What if you can't *fix* Gunther? You never gonna talk to her again?" Quinn asked.

"I will. Just not right now."

"Okay, Quinn. Call Cara." Susanna shot a stern look at Jake and handed the phone to her husband.

Susanna made French toast and bacon for breakfast. Quinn chattered basketball scores, baseball line-ups, and trades. Jake couldn't concentrate. He wanted Cara's help but was afraid she'd be angry with him. *Did I break Grace's heart? Probably.* Still, finding out she was the Movie Maven was such a shock, he was still getting used to the idea and dreading the pictures that would appear in a couple of days in *Celebs 'R Us,* and in the newspapers, too.

He wondered how the anger in his gut looked spilling all over his face and all over the centerspread of the magazine. The thought of what he looked like made him shudder. And Grace. Her pitiful face—so shocked, upset, sad, and imploring. And could he forgive her? No, he couldn't, he didn't.

He closed his eyes as the expression of deep hurt on her face reappeared in his mind. Those baby blues, once filled with laughter, happiness, desire, paled underneath the heavy burden of sadness. He'd never forget her eyes.

Asshole. I made everything worse. Now she hates me. Do I still love her? Maybe. Can I trust her? Doubt it. His pain intensified as these thoughts swirled around his mind and heart while he pretended to be listening to Quinn.

Cara arrived after they finished breakfast. Susanna offered her food. "Thanks, but I just ate. What's this about?"

Quinn started the explanation, and then Jake jumped in. "Grace told you…uh…why she attacked Gunther, right?"

Cara nodded, her mouth compressed into a thin line. "He deserved it and more."

"What happened? We're in the dark here," Quinn piped up.

"I can't say, Quinn. Grace swore me to secrecy."

"Great! I'm working in the dark." He threw his hands up.

"I have an idea. Let me make a phone call," Cara said.

The others sat by quietly, watching her while she dialed. "Tiffany Cowles, please. Cara Brewster. Yes, I'll hold." She got up and walked across the room to the window. "Tiffany? Hi. Remember when you said if I ever needed anything? Actually, I do. It's about Gunther Quill."

Cara glanced at the others, who were listening to her conversation. She slowly walked into the dining room, out of earshot.

Susanna got up and turned on some music. "Let's give her some privacy."

****

Grace moped around the house on Monday. Cara was out, Grant was working, and Sarah was at school. She missed Jake and wondered what he was doing on his day off. At the window, she spied the first robin of spring. Whipping out her phone, she went to text Jake but stopped.

I can't tell him about a robin. He's not my boyfriend any more. I can't text him about anything. She heaved a deep and lonely sigh as she perched on the window seat, watching the sun trying to break through. Grace wracked her brain, attempting to think of ways to patch up her relationship with Jake. He had become almost as important to her as the air she breathed.

Only now did she see how much she turned to him first, thought of him first with a new idea, something she saw, a laugh, of any kind, or when she needed advice. She'd come to depend on his being there.

And as for affection and physical love, well, Jake was unequaled. She missed snuggling up against his warm body in bed. And his touch, good morning kiss, bear hugs…all parts of them together she had taken for granted. And lovemaking…well there weren't words for how much she missed their intimacy. Now it was all gone, and while the world was coming into spring, Grace was entering a cold and solitary season of her life.

There were no more tears left. Unhappiness had morphed into sadness, regret, and anger at herself for her behavior. *Why didn't I believe he'd forgive me? Why didn't I tell him when we talked about Gunther? That would have been the perfect time. He was in a forgiving mood. How can I blame him for not trusting me? I can't. If he had kept such a big secret from me, I'd feel the same.*

At eleven, she started preparing lunch. Although she didn't know where Cara went or when she'd be back, she knew her sister had to eat. She pulled out some leftover chicken, grapes, cranberries, and walnuts and began making chicken salad. A little music on the radio seemed to help, until they played Matthew Morrison singing *Summer Rain*. The song made her think of making love with Jake. She shut it off and ignored the watering of her eyes.

As she was stirring in the walnuts, she heard the front door creak. "I'm home," Cara called out.

Licking a little mayonnaise off her fingers, Grace met her sister in the hallway. "Lunch is ready. Where'd you go?"

"I'm starved." Cara walked into the kitchen. Grace sensed she was avoiding the question. Cara set the table while Grace portioned out the tasty salad on a small bed of lettuce on each plate. A few slices of French bread and two glasses of mint iced tea finished off the meal.

"This looks great. Thank you, Pookie."

"Pookie? Uh oh." Cara cocked her head slightly when she raised her gaze to her sister. "That means you have bad news."

"Does it?"

"You never noticed? You always call me 'Pookie' when you have to tell me something bad."

"Okay, okay," Cara took a forkful of salad and sat chewing while looking at Grace.

Grace sipped her tea. Her appetite had suddenly gone south. After swallowing, Cara launched into the story about Gunther's call to Jake and his reaching out to her for help.

"That scumbag! After what he did to me?" Grace rose out of her chair and paced.

"I fixed it." Grace slowly resumed her seat. "You did?"

Cara nodded.

"How?"

"I called Tiffany." She smiled.

"Tiffany Cowles? You didn't!" Grace's mouth hung open.

"I did. She and I are friends, sort of."

"And?"

"She's going to call Gunther and tell him to back off or else."

"Or else what?"

"I didn't get into details. But it's pretty crazy to buck Tiffany."

"Don't I know it." Gracie looked at her cuticles.

"She didn't mean to get Gunther on your back. Said she was teaching you a lesson."

"I didn't want to write any more of those nasty reviews. I'm not a nasty person."

"I know, Pookie," Cara patted Grace's hand. "She's running your glowing review of Jake's movie, though it's killing her," she chuckled.

"Yeah?"

"To make it up to you."

"Sweet." Grace smiled. *Good for Jake.* "Did he say anything about us?"

"Jake?" Cara shook her head. "I didn't ask, since you told me to butt out."

"Damn," she muttered.

Cara faced her sister and grabbed her shoulder. "Look! He cared enough about you to take this Gunther thing to Quinn and me."

"Oh, God! He didn't tell Quinn about Gunther?"

"Of course not. Neither did I."

Grace let out a big breath.

"Obviously he cares for you."

"But I destroyed what we had." Grace hung her head, her fingers played with the hem of her sweater.

"So rebuild."

"Easy to say…"

"Grant and I did."

"You two were together for a long time. Have a kid…it's not the same."

"Do you love him?"

Grace nodded.

"Then try, Pookie. Try." Cara pushed to her feet. Grace cleared the table. "Let me do those. You made lunch."

"I don't have anything to do." Grace turned on the faucet.

"Find something. Read a book. Scoot," Cara said, shooing her sister out of the room.

Grace went back to the window to see the sun poking through the gray clouds. She smiled. Her cell rang. The familiar song, *Summer Rain*, tinkled through the apartment. *Maybe it's Jake?* She picked up the phone only to spy a strange number. A frown wrinkled her forehead as she spoke.

"Grace? Max Webster here."

"The producer?"

"None other. About your screenplay. I love it. Can we meet?"

"Sure, sure. When?"

"How about lunch tomorrow? Say one at Limoges? Do you know where it is?"

"I do. I'll be there. And thanks."

"A pleasure."

He hung up. A zing shot through her body, and she went to call Jake but put the brakes on when his number came up. *I can't call him. But I can't not tell him. That's keeping stuff from him...again. But he's not my...but he did tell me...damn. Text him, Grace.*

She sat down on the sofa and composed a text. After she hit *send*, she ran into the kitchen to tell her sister. As she was babbling on, her phone dinged. This time it was Jake.

> *Great news about your play. Congratulations. Hope Max buys it and pays you a boatload of money. Good luck.*

Her smile melted into a frown as she noticed there was no *love* at the end of the message. *Just as if he were only a friend.* A heaviness lodged in her chest and breathing became difficult. She blinked back tears but couldn't look Cara in the eye.

"Bad news?"

"Not good news." Grace excused herself and retreated to her room. She shut the door and collapsed on the bed. *It's over, Grace. Face it. O-v-e-r. You screwed up. He's gone.*

After slipping between the sheets, Graced switched off the light. She lay for a while with her eyes open, staring into the darkness. Her mind couldn't take in that Jake was out of her life. *I can never be friends with him because I'll never stop wanting him.* The pain in her heart was like mourning for the loss of a loved one. *It's like a death.* She sighed and tossed for a while, looking for a comfortable position. Finally, grief wore her out, and she fell into a fitful rest.

The next day, Grace dressed in a wool skirt and sweater and set out to walk to Limoges. It was a warm day for the end of March, and she turned her face up to the sun as she strolled down Central Park West. Her heart beat slowed under the weight of her emotions. She couldn't let go of Jake. Stopping on a bench, she warred with herself whether to text Jake or not. *He said something about having a talk. So it's okay to ask about that.*

She typed out her message about meeting, but her shaky hand hung back when it was time to press the send button. *If he says no, then I'll let it go…let him go? I don't know if I can. May have no choice.* She debated if she could take a negative response from him or not. Was this the time, just before meeting with Max to put herself out there? So many questions. Then she closed her eyes and hit *send* before she could chicken out. *I have to know. Have to do this. Even if it's bad.*

Standing up on wobbly legs, Grace continued on her walk. She could see Limoges through the trees. The sound of the ding, alerting her to the arrival of a text, made her suck in air.

Yes. Want to talk. Sunday afternoon?

She let out her breath and allowed a small smile to stretch her lips. *There's hope!*

Sunday's good. What time?

She stopped to wait until the sound of a message arriving came again a few seconds later.

Dinner at seven? My place or Panama?

Panama had become their new favorite restaurant.

You pick.

Okay. Here. Order in Chinese?

Perfect.

How was she going to wait until Sunday? A glance at her watch told her if she didn't make tracks quickly, she'd be late to meet Max. *Crap!* Picking up the pace, Grace's step had lightened a bit at the thought of meeting with Jake. *And if we're at his place, maybe I can seduce him into...Stop! Honest talk. Nothing more. Yeah, right.* Her smile got bigger at the thought of being in his arms again.

Before she knew it, she was at the front door of Limoges then being shown to Max Webster's table.

* * * *

Quinn tried to give Jake advice about Grace, but Susanna interrupted and told him to discount what her husband said. Jake laughed but listened when Susanna sat him down.

"She's coming over tonight?"

"Yeah. To talk." He rested his palms on his thighs.

"What are you going to say?"

"I don't know. Haven't heard from her since the dance contest."

"She's probably waiting for you to say something."

"Great." He hung his head.

"Do you love her? Sorry for being so personal..."

"No, no, that's all right. Yeah. I do. Miss her like crazy. But the trust thing is a problem."

"Can you tell her you need her to be honest with you...all the time?"

"I can tell her but my saying and her doing, well..." He joined and unjoined his fingers. "How will I know for sure if she's being honest?"

"You won't."

"See? That's my dilemma. What if it were about another guy? I'd go nuts."

"Do you think she'd do that?"

He shook his head. "She'd never two-time me."

"You sound so sure."

"She's had chances. She knows…about my past. That would be the end. It'd kill me."

"If you're so sure of that, then why are you hesitating?"

"She says she was afraid to tell me, but when it came out, I was madder than I'd have been if she'd told me. At least I think I was."

"She was afraid you'd be mad, and then you were mad. What's wrong here?"

"What?"

"She was right. You were mad, twice as mad. Probably confirmed her decision not to tell you."

"Never saw it like that."

"Maybe it's the way she saw it?"

"Thanks, Susanna." Jake gave her a hug and headed home, feeling stronger than he had for days. *Gracie, will you come back to me?* As he walked, he wondered if his silence hadn't hardened her resolve to leave him. *Stupid!* His palms began to sweat and the collar of his shirt seemed to tighten.

Jake kept himself busy arranging for singing and dancing lessons in addition to his evenings and matinée performances. Sunday came soon enough. After the afternoon show, he raced home to clean house. He ordered Grace's favorite dishes from The Yangtse, their local Chinese restaurant. Fried dumplings, hot and sour soup, and crispy prawns with walnuts were on the way.

He took a shower and brushed his teeth. *Sex? Tonight? Hope so, but maybe not. Still should be prepared.* He checked the night stand for condoms. *His pulse kicked up at the idea of getting her back in his bed.* It had already been too long. Jake was horny, itchy to touch and kiss her.

Talk! Gonna talk first. He tried to calm his libido, but it was a struggle. *If she comes in dressed sexy, it's all over for me.* He laughed at his own weakness. *If I want her that much, does it mean I love her? Or is it only lust? Maybe both.*

He chuckled as he slapped on *Macho,* his favorite aftershave. He stroked his cheek. He'd managed to shave it down to just the right length for his stubble to be sexy but not annoying. Keeping it the right length was a chore, but he was getting better at it. *Gracie likes some growth on my face.* He smiled into the mirror. *Don't hate me, baby.*

The buzzer sounded as he was pulling a T-shirt over his head. He pressed the buzzer and a serious set of nerves kicked in. He was sweating, breathing heavy, and couldn't stand still. All the signs he was in love. *Ugh. Gotta be cool. Rational.*

He opened the door. She looked up, and their eyes locked. He saw fear, and his heart melted. *Don't be afraid of me, Gracie. Please.*

"Come in, Come in."

She shed her coat, and he hung it on a hook.

When she turned to face him, she was wearing a big sweater that fell off one shoulder. It was midnight blue, bringing out the color of her eyes. He could see her jiggle. *No bra.* He swallowed as his gaze slid down her body, from the sweater to the tight, light blue jeans hugging her hips and flaring at the bottom in a flattering boot cut style. His mouth went dry as he mentally stripped her naked. *Stop! Talk. Need to talk.*

He took her hand and led her to the little table that was his dining room.

"Dinner. All your favorites." He opened container after container. Tempting aromas of Chinese delicacies filled the air. His stomach growled. *Feed one appetite at a time. Talk!* Controlling his sex drive was going to be a bigger problem than he anticipated. *How can I ever forget making love to her? She's so tempting.*

"Thanks. I'm not very hungry." Grace put two dumplings on her plate and two shrimp.

"No soup? It's so cold outside."

"Yeah, but…I'm not hungry." She nibbled on her food, watching him chow down.

Then he opened a container of soup and tasted it. "Ow, hot but good."

"You okay?"

He nodded, touching his lip gingerly. *I love it when she takes care of me. Stop! Talk. Only talk. She talks. I listen.*

"You wanted to talk," she began, picking up her dumpling with chopsticks.

"Yeah. I thought we should. I mean…what happened. Seemed to blow us apart and…well…I don't—" He stopped. *What should I say?*

"Go on."

"I don't know what to say."

"Tell me what you want. Do you want to break up? Become only friends? Or stay together?" Her face paled as she spoke. She was so white, he thought she'd faint.

"Are you all right, Grace? Do you want to lie down? You're awfully pale."

"Lie down? Trying to get me into bed?" Her eyes flashed.

"Of course not. I thought you were going to pass out. Are you sick?" *Getting you into bed would be heaven.*

"I'm not sick. I…I was feeling a little weak for a moment."

"Maybe you need food."

"I'm fine."

"Glass of wine? I have your favorite brand, Velvet Vineyards."

"Trying to get me drunk so I'll sleep with you?" She cocked an eyebrow at him.

"What's going on? These are innocent remarks."

"Trying to tell me you don't want to sleep with me."

"I didn't say that."

"Then you do want to sleep with me."

"What happened to our talk?" Helplessness overcame Jake. Nothing he said came out right.

"Do you want to sleep with me?"

"Of course. You know that."

"Do I? Do I? I don't hear from you for a week and…" Grace broke down. She hid her face with her hands, but Jake saw the wetness.

He was destroyed. He had made her cry. In a heartbeat, he was beside her, taking her into his arms. "Don't cry, Gracie. Baby, don't cry."

"I don't know what to think. I'm confused," she wailed.

"So am I."

"You're so cold, then you buy my favorite foods and you're so nice...what is it, nice or cold? Love or hate?"

He held her to him and stroked her hair. Grace snaked her arms around his middle and hugged him, burying her face in his chest, wetting his T-shirt with her tears.

"I don't hate you, Gracie, honey. I could never hate you."

"But you don't love me."

"Can we try this talk again? Can we talk about trust?"

"Okay. Trust." Grace wiped her eyes with her hand and sat back, easing away from Jake.

"Yeah. I trusted you, and now I've lost a lotta that trust. I don't know if you're going to hide stuff from me because you're afraid it'll make me mad."

"I promise never to do that again."

"Are you afraid when I get mad? Do I scare you?"

She nodded. "But not afraid the way you think. Afraid you'll...stop..." She took a deep shuddering breath, "Stop loving me."

"Oh, baby," he reached for her. "Anger wouldn't make me do that. Sure I was mad you, said nasty things. But what got me was you didn't trust me enough to tell me before. Then I had to be humiliated in the press. Told in front of the world...something you should have told me in private."

"That was wrong. I'm sorry."

"Did you see our pictures in *Celebs 'R Us?* And the newspapers?"

"They were awful. I'm so sorry, Jake. I had no idea...I'll never do that again."

"Even if what you're going to tell me might make me mad?"

Her voice shook. "I'll try. That's hard for me. I'm not good with anger."

Jake reached out and took her hand.

"You'd never lie about...seeing another man. Would you?"

"I'd never see anyone else while I'm committed to you. Never. No matter what."

He breathed a sigh of relief. That idea had been nagging at the back of his mind all week, and he didn't know how to ask. The words simply tumbled out as they often did with Jake. This time he didn't make a mess of it, but managed to speak from his heart. "And I'm sorry, too."

"For what?"

"For treating you so badly…for making you so mad at me, that you…you…did that."

He offered her his handkerchief. She wiped her face then took a bite of her dumpling. "I overreacted."

"I had it coming." He hung his head. Grace cupped his cheek then kissed it. He took the opportunity to brush her lips with his.

"Maybe we should start again. We rushed into living together."

"That was your idea." She finished her dumpling.

"I know. Still. Could we date?" *Come on, Gracie. Don't leave me.*

Grace hesitated. She took a deep breath and looked him squarely in the eye before she spoke. "I don't want to be without you. There, I've said it. I'll go back to dating, if it means we can be together."

Jake scooped her into his arms and kissed her passionately. "I love you, Gracie," he whispered. "I want us to be together."

Color suffused her pale face, and a smile stretched her lips. "Could you put some of that shrimp and rice on my plate. Guess I'm hungry after all." They ate in silence, eyeing each other hungrily while they shoveled in the delicious food. Gracie smiled. "Did you see the whole review of your new movie?"

"Yours? You mean the Movie Maven's?"

"Uh huh."

"I did. It was awesome. Thank you."

"I loved the movie. First nice review Tiffany agreed to print. I'm done with the Movie Maven, by the way."

"Good." He finished the container of hot and sour soup.

"Did you see the piece Tiffany put in her gossip column about Gunther?"

He shook his head.

"Here. I've got it right here." She handed Jake the piece cut from the magazine

To a certain producer. We know what you're up to. No more mistreatment of young women. Or

we will out you. Right here. Trust me, we mean it. You know who you are.

"Do you think it'll stop him?"

She shrugged. "I don't know. No more time for dumb Movie Maven stuff anyway." She took a mouthful of the shrimp and rice. He raised his eyebrows in a questioning glance. She smiled mysteriously at him. "Max Webster bought my screenplay."

Jake jumped up from the table. "He did? Wow! Fantastic!"

"He's sending the contract over tomorrow. I've got to go to L.A. for script meetings. He says we have to change a bunch of stuff, and I've got to be there."

"You're going to LA? When?"

"Don't know yet. In a few weeks. Not until the contract is signed, of course."

A pain shot through his chest. "I thought we'd have time."

"We have some. Don't know how much." Gracie finished the food on her plate.

Jake had made up his mind. "Move in."

"What about the trust thing...taking it slow and all?"

"Thought I had all the time in the world. Now that you're leaving...we covered it all. I want to spend every second I can with you before you go." He swallowed the last bite of shrimp.

"Let me think about it."

"Please, Gracie." He brushed his lips against the back of her hand. "Do you love me?"

"I do. I do love you, but I don't want to get my heart broken again."

"I promise not to break your heart. Say you will." He kissed up her arm to her bare shoulder, where he nibbled gently. "Please. We were so good," he whispered.

"Okay, okay. You convinced me," she mumbled, her eyes closing.

Jake pulled her out of her chair and waltzed her around the small apartment. Then he hugged her tight and stroked her hair. "Your script will make an awesome movie."

"Thank you for sending it to Max."

"Susanna did that."

"Take the credit, Jake. You deserve it. Thank you also for saving me from Gunther."

He held her at arm's length. "What?"

"Cara told me."

"She was supposed to keep it a secret." He frowned.

"No secrets between sisters. Besides…didn't we just say *no secrets*?"

He laughed. "Suppose we did. Couldn't have Gunther wrecking your life any more than he already did."

"You're the best." She pulled him to her for a deep kiss as she pressed her hips against his.

God I want her. His libido was going crazy as he folded her into his embrace and probed her mouth passionately.

"Wearing anything under that sweater?" He breathed into her ear.

"Nope."

His lips grazed her bare shoulder while his fingers closed over her breast.

"Gracie," he murmured, losing himself in her delicious lilac scent and warm softness. She stepped closer to him and sighed.

Chapter Eleven

Grace's head was spinning. *Moving in with Jake, screenplay sold, moving back to L.A.*

Happiness filled her heart as excitement sent tingles up her spine. She'd be taking her own place in the movie world as a screenwriter, and she'd have Jake by her side. *But what happens when I leave?* She pushed that negative thought out of her mind. *I've been so depressed, just want to be happy now.* She turned her attention to the handsome man nibbling on her shoulder and the sensations he was creating.

She dipped her fingers underneath his T-shirt and slid them up his smooth skin, pressing her fingertips into his muscles. He made a small sound deep in his throat, which made her smile. *He always loved my touch.* Resting her palm on his back, she sensed the power there and it excited her. *To have him on top of me, loving me again. Heaven.*

"Gracie…do you want to…"

"Yes," she responded firmly and quickly. Jake backed away from her and returned to the sofa, which was his pull-out bed. In less than two minutes he had it converted to a place for making love. He led her to it. Before lying down, he stripped her sweater off and tossed it on a chair.

With his gaze glued to her chest, Jake ripped his T-shirt over his head. He unbuttoned her jeans first then his own. With one hand on each side of her, he slid the garment down, revealing her black satin bikini panties underneath.

"Wow. Forgot about those. You look…amazing." His hungry eyes feasted on her body. Suddenly bashful, Grace folded her arms across her chest.

His eyebrows rose in surprise. "Shy? Now?"

"Drop those drawers, Mister," she directed, pointing to his jeans. Jake shed them and his boxers quickly.

"Better," she said, just before her mouth went dry. She loved looking at his perfect form and simply the sight of him naked caused her pulse to kick up. He ran his fingers up and over her breasts, then down again before pulling her into his embrace. His lips sought hers as he angled his head to deepen the kiss. His mouth possessed hers with an urgency and a passion she had not seen before. His thrilling desire melted her in his arms.

Pulling her in tight, he slipped his leg between hers, making her gasp.

"You okay?"

"Oh, God, yes, better than okay," she muttered, closing her eyes as he pushed against her with ever-increasing pressure. His hands came around behind her, gliding down her back until they reached her bottom. Jake took hold and squeezed, drawing her flush with his rapidly growing erection. She shivered as her breasts flattened against his hard pecs.

He cradled her in his arms, lowering her to the bed. He lay next to her and explored her body, starting at her shoulders and working his way down. His mouth followed, stopping at her breasts to feed, sucking and nipping. His voracious appetite for her took her breath away. If she needed convincing that he loved her, his actions told her volumes.

"The most beautiful sight in the world," he muttered, staring at her. He parted her legs and crouched between them, lowering himself to his knees. Gracie combed his hair off his forehead with her fingers before cupping his face. She bent at the waist, rising to plant her lips on his in a hungry kiss.

She wanted to consume him, to join them completely as one. He curled his fingers around her thighs, while his thumbs teased her core. A shudder rocketed through her. Gooseflesh broke out on her skin as he kissed his way down her chest and over her abdomen.

Before she could say or do anything, his head was between her legs. At the first touch of his tongue, her back arched and she groaned. He raised his head, and their gazes locked for a moment. Then, smiling, he returned to giving her pleasure so intense she thought she'd pass out.

Her senses took over, driving all rational thought from her mind. All she could do was feel the excitement he was creating spiraling up and up…winding up her muscles like a top, spinning dangerously close to out-of-control.

All attempts at speech failed as Grace shut her eyes and gave in to the burning heat coursing through her veins. Riding the tide of desire like a magic carpet, she exploded in a powerful orgasm, fireworks going off inside her. Tiny sparks of satisfaction were blown all the way to her fingers and toes as she finally relaxed.

"Holy Hell," she murmured, her eyes still closed as Jake moved away from her.

"Good?"

"Beyond good, beyond great, beyond amazing." She cracked her eyelids open to spy a big, shit-eating grin on his face. "Proud of yourself?" she asked.

He nodded as he reached into the nightstand drawer and withdrew a condom. Gracie curled her fingers around his erection, which appeared bigger than ever and as hard as granite. Her eyes widened as he made quick work of the wrapper, sat back on his haunches, and covered himself.

"Roll over." She arched her eyebrows in question. "Something a little different…to start."

She rolled onto her stomach and allowed him to position her, raising her butt in the air. Turning her head to the side, she was barely able to see him rise up on his knees before he gripped her hips. Her wetness allowed him to slip inside her quickly and easily. He pulled her up flat against him. Each groaned as they were joined.

Grace braced herself, keeping her position steady while Jake pounded into her. "Oh, God, Gracie," he moaned as he plunged in faster and faster. Once again her body took flight, surprising her with the force of her response.

After a few more hard thrusts, she climaxed a second time, groaning into the pillow. Then, abruptly, he stopped. "Turn over," he commanded, and she obeyed. He raised her knees before entering her. She hooked one leg around his waist and lifted the other one high to rest on his shoulder.

"Oh my God," Jake muttered, as he penetrated deeper into her and moved in and out faster and harder. She brushed her fingers through his chest hair before resting her hands on his shoulders. Gracie studied his face. A sexual flush started in his chest and rose halfway up his neck. His eyes were slits but rays of desire shot from them like sparks. His lips were parted slightly. *God when he's inside me, it feels so great. He fills me completely.*

She didn't have long to watch him as his release gripped him, making sweat break out on his forehead and a long, passionate groan leave his lips as his hips thrust one more time before stopping. The look of ecstasy on his face made her smile.

"Oh, Gracie," he murmured, collapsing on her, their sweaty chests slipping and sliding against each other. She ran her nails over the fine layer of moisture on his back and sucked on his skin, enjoying the taste of saltiness mingling with the flavor of Jake.

"What sweetheart?" she asked.

"You took me someplace I've never been before."

Jake slid off her and sprinted to the bathroom. He returned quickly to nestle by her side, holding her close. She rested her head on his shoulder.

"You're the most amazing lover. That was…a roller coaster to heaven."

He laughed. "Such a writer!" He ran his hand gently and lovingly over her chest, down to her hip, where it rested while the forefinger of his other hand lazily drew circles around her breasts.

"You are the most beautiful woman I've ever made love to."

"Really? And the number of women is…high?"

Jake blushed. "Oops. Shut up, Jake," he said.

"No, really. You've opened up this topic again. How many?"

"I lost track…" He blushed deeper, "I mean, I didn't keep count."

"How many, approximately?"

"Plenty. Enough to let you know how extraordinary you are."

"Since you're so shy, how did you get all these women?"

"Women love shy guys. Don't see us coming then…wham! They're naked." He chuckled. "Seriously? Women are attracted to shy guys. Being in road companies for regional theater…easy to meet new women. Kinda like a kid in a candy store."

"Oh?" She cocked an eyebrow at him.

"You're the best ever. I got to be pretty good…all that practice."

"Good? You think you're good?" His face fell. "You're not good, you're spectacular!" She kissed his lips then cuddled into him. "But no more sleeping around, okay?"

"Oh, I stopped, long ago."

"You grew up?" She ran her finger down his chest.

"Might say that. Too many girls with gorilla big brothers." He kissed her shoulder.

"Find it hard to see you as a seducer."

"Even after the way I came on to you?"

"Well, maybe."

"I wasn't a seducer. Just cashed in on being an actor. But it got boring."

"You expect me to believe that?" She rested her palm on his chest.

"Now the only woman I want in my bed is you." He leaned over and planted a sweet kiss on her lips. *Music to my ears.* "I'll try to make you happy, happy enough so you don't need anyone else," he said.

Gotta love this guy. "That's beautiful."

"You make me happier than I thought possible, honey. Stay with me always." He kissed her hair.

She stroked his cheek. "I'll stay as long as I can."

They lingered until nine o'clock, when Jake accompanied her to Cara's place to gather her things. He chatted with Cara and Grant while Grace packed up. As she was packing, Grace realized this was no ordinary moving out. This would be permanent.

First, she'd be living with Jake, then she'd return to Los Angeles and take up residence in the house she had shared with Cara. Cara would be staying in New York to continue her Broadway run and marry Grant. Who knew when she'd return to the West Coast? By then, Grace would probably have her own place.

Even if she stayed at Cara's, life for them would not be the same. Grace realized it was time to cut her ties from her sibling, or at least loosen them. Feeling stronger than ever, Gracie knew she was ready, but she wasn't sure about her sister. "Cara, can I talk to you in the kitchen?"

The actress pushed to her feet. Her face grim, she shot a look at Grant, before joining Gracie.

"You know Max Webster was interested in my screenplay."

"Did he make you an offer?"

She nodded. "He's sending over a contract."

"I'll have Gordon Lesser look it over."

"Thanks, I'd appreciate it."

"Or maybe someone in Grant's firm. Gee, now that we're together, I might have to go there for a good entertainment lawyer." She chewed her lip.

"I'm moving out, Cara."

"I know, Pookie. To live with Jake."

"Longer than that. Max said in a couple of weeks, script conferences will start, and I'll have to be in Los Angeles."

"Okay. You do that for a few weeks then come back to New York, right?"

Grace shook her head. "I don't plan to come back. Not for a long time."

"So you're saying...?"

"It's time for us to separate, Carol Anne." The intimate conversation made using her sister's real name, not her stage name, more appropriate. Cara looked down at her fingernails. Grace could see her eyelashes working fast and knew she was upset. "This had to come sooner or later."

"Doesn't make it any easier."

Grace stepped closer, running her hand up and down Cara's arm. "You have your own family now. This is what you've always wanted...to be with Grant and Sarah."

"But no one replaces you."

"No one will replace you, either. It's time for me to stand on my own. I've made a ton of mistakes this year. I need to get myself together. This may be my one chance. I have to take it."

"I'd never stand in your way, Pookie. You've been such an important part of my life for so long...I..."

"And you, mine. I know you wouldn't. Time for me to sink or swim. You can't always bail me out...like with Gunther Quill..."

"That lowlife, creep. I've withdrawn from his picture."

"Cara! Don't do that on account of me!"

"How can I look him in the eye every day when I know what he's done to you?"

"You shouldn't have done that. That picture was a good opportunity for you."

"Grant's thrilled. Means I'm staying in the show longer, will be in New York."

"It's your career. I don't want to interfere…"

"You're not. It was my decision."

"I'll be at the house for a while. Is that okay?"

"Of course! It's your home, too. You won't be my secretary anymore?"

Grace patted her sister's arm. "I'm not leaving you in the lurch. I'll still take care of the house, your finances, and stuff. Maybe you need to look for someone here to help you out."

"You won't be here to help me plan my wedding!" A look of panic crossed Cara's face. "Will you be here when I get married?"

"Of course! I wouldn't miss that! I'm hoping to be a bridesmaid. I'll help you plan as much as I can from L.A."

"A bridesmaid, yes. Maid of Honor. I'm having it at Limoges…"

"I can work with Jean Marc over the phone."

"Thank you, Pookie." Cara hugged her sister. A few tears broke through Cara's defenses. Grace wiped them with her thumb.

"I love you, Cara. You're the best. Thank you for everything."

"Good luck, Pook. I'm here if you need me."

The women hugged again, and Carol Anne let out a brief sob. When she recovered, they left the kitchen, strolling arm-in-arm.

"Are you ready?" Jake stood up. Grace nodded. Grant stepped forward to hug Grace and wish her good luck. Jake kissed Cara's cheek and shook hands with Grant. With Jake toting the suitcases, the young lovers returned to his apartment and a new beginning.

* * * *

At first, Grace tiptoed around the place, afraid to put something in the wrong spot or to leave her things lying around. Scared if she did something wrong, Jake would ask her to leave. But every night he slung his arm around her as they walked home, planning their late night meal, he was full of smiles and laughter. In fact, Grace had never seen him more cheerful.

Her grins never stopped. Small day-to-day annoyances didn't bother her. She'd even forgotten about Gunther Quill. *This is the life I'm meant to lead.*

After two weeks, she moved around the apartment as if she belonged there. She learned the kitchen quickly and made some changes to suit her style. She did most of the cooking, though Jake made a mean French toast on his day off. He did the dishes, vacuumed, and changed the sheets. Grace cleaned the bathroom.

During the day, she worked on a new screenplay while he was at singing lessons and dance classes. "I need to be ready for anything. A great musical might come my way." Jake's new determination to master all aspects of his craft impressed her.

After Grace's glowing review, he got a call from Skip, now his agent too, that a few producers and directors had inquired about him. Jake received a few scripts from Skip, which he shared with Grace. They read them together, snuggled up on the sofa like two puppies, and then compared notes.

The iciness of winter began to melt in April as white snow drops and lavender crocuses, courageous early flowers, bloomed in New York City. Grace dragged Jake to Central Park for long walks. Bright yellow daffodils were up and ready to burst. Hints of yellow dotted fenced-in fields where forsythia, a few daffs, and jonquils received enough sun to blossom.

She led him to the spots where there were the most flowers blooming. The brilliant, new colors refreshed her spirit. They held hands and soon Jake shared her enthusiasm for exploring deeper and deeper in Central Park. It became a place where they could be alone together with nature, listening to bird songs and being in love. A place beyond the prying eyes of the press.

He bought her a romantic lunch at The Boathouse, where they huddled together at a table by the window, sipping coffee. Grace pulled her fleece jacket around her shoulders to ward off the chill seeping through the worn seams of the old windows.

"I love this place," Jake said, glancing around.

"The lake is beautiful, even when it's still cold outside."

He laced his fingers with hers. "You're beautiful, too." Grace looked down and smiled. *He's so sweet.* They sat holding hands for another half hour before they returned home.

However, not all days were sunshine and sweetness, sometimes they argued.

"Where'd you put the laundry soap?" A crease formed between his brows.

"Here," Gracie said, opening the pantry door and pointing to a container next to the laundry basket.

"I always keep it in the lower cabinet. I spent all morning looking for it! Now it's too late to do laundry before I have to go to the theater!"

"Next to the laundry basket makes more sense than that cabinet."

"But that's where it always was!"

"If you don't want me here, I'll just…"

"I didn't *say* I didn't want you here. I said I wanted the laundry detergent in the cabinet."

"Fine!" Grace shouted as she slammed the cabinet door after she replaced the detergent.

"Don't slam that. You might break it!" He hollered back.

"Then close it yourself!" She walked away in a huff. *This living together sucks sometimes.*

Evenings were always good. They made love almost every night. Then they curled up together cuddling and snuggling until daybreak. In the morning, she hated to leave the toasty bed and the warm body of her lover. Jake was affectionate, hugging, kissing, and touching her often. She relaxed and grew confident under the warmth of his love.

Once the contract with Max Webster was signed, and a script doctor was hired, Grace's Eden was about to end. The time for her to go had arrived. She hesitated telling Jake, delaying until after the show. The air was still chilly in mid-April. They were walking home hand-in-hand when she figured the time was right.

"Max found a script doctor for my screenplay."

"Oh?" Jake stopped and turned toward her.

"They want me there in a week."

"You're leaving?"

She nodded. "We knew this day would come."

"I suppose. Guess I'd hoped something would hold things up."

"Like maybe not making the movie?"

"I'd never wish that…a delay…something. Hope against hope." His face clouded over.

"I hate to leave." Grace looked away from him so he couldn't see the glint of tears in her eyes. *He hates it when women cry.*

"Do you?" He stopped, grabbing her arms, forcing her to face him. She nodded as emotion trapped her words in her throat. He tipped her chin up so she couldn't avoid his stare. "Are you crying?"

"I know how you hate crying women."

"Yeah. It tears me up. But if you wanna cry…"

She shook her head. "I'm happy to make this dream a reality…but I hate leaving you."

He blew out a breath. "Truth."

Grace hugged him around the waist, burying her face in his jacket. Tears flowed. A muffled "I love you" stole from her mouth. Jake closed his arms around her, holding her close.

"I love you, too, Gracie." He rested his chin on her head.

"Hey, buddy, get a room!" A man shot at them as he walked by.

Jake chuckled. "Yeah. We have a room. Let's go home," He separated from her and took her hand.

Home? I love the sound of that. He tossed her his handkerchief as they continued up the avenue.

By the time they reached his building, she had dried her tears. As they climbed the stairs of the brownstone, Jake brought up the topic again. "How long will you be gone?"

"I don't know. We have to fix the script, then casting. I don't know when shooting's scheduled…maybe months."

"Months? Like two, four? I can handle that. As long as it isn't years."

"Years? No way!" She shook her head.

"Can you handle it, Gracie? You'll be working with guys. Sets can be seductive."

"You know all about that, right?"

Jake blushed. "Never said I was an angel."

"Wouldn't have believed you if you had," she snickered.

"Oh?" He tackled her around the waist and threw her down underneath him on the sofa. His mouth closed down on hers, possessing her. She softened against him, molding her body to his. When he came up for air, he stared at her. She saw questions, lust, and concern in his liquid gold eyes.

"What?"

"How many nights before you go?" he asked.

"Seven."

He ripped his T-shirt over his head. "Why are we wasting time?" Only a few minutes passed before the lovers had stripped down and were entwined in each other's arms. Grace pushed thoughts of her departure out of her head and focused on Jake. Happiness bubbled up in her chest as passion took over.

In her heart, appreciation for what she had warred with the greediness of wanting more. She tried to appear grateful but couldn't deny the empty feeling in her chest when she thought of leaving Jake. The price she was paying to have her dream weighed heavily on her.

Grace kept her spirits up, focusing on the positive as often as possible without sounding silly or unrealistic. Doubt about the survival of their relationship never left the back of her mind, though she refused to dwell on it and spoil their last few days together.

On her last day, Grace tried to slow life down, to remember every second, every thought, every word. Bobby was driving her to the airport, and Cara, Grant and Sarah were coming to see her off. Jake stood next to her as Bobby loaded her suitcases in the limo.

"Remember our deal," he whispered.

"Faithful for four months."

"Right. And after that?"

"If tempted, call." Grace drew closer to him.

"Right. Good, baby." He wound his arms around her.

She raised her chin, and he captured her mouth in a greedy kiss. It wasn't long before Bobby and Grant were making noises, so the lovers split.

"Hey, guys, last one for a while." Then everyone else kissed Grace, who burst into tears when Sarah started to cry.

Bobby opened the back door. "If you don't get in the car and go, there'll be a flood," he said. Grace slid inside and raised her hand to the window. Jake stood up against the car.

"I love you, Gracie. Don't ever forget that!"

"I won't." Bobby threw the car in gear, and they moved into the avenue and picked up speed, heading uptown. Gracie remained twisted around, looking out the back window until she couldn't see them anymore. Heaviness settled in her chest.

"If it's meant to be, it'll last, Gracie."

"I hope you're right." The ache in her chest pounded harder. "Right now it hurts like hell."

"I get it. Peg and I were separated, too."

"How?"

"I was in the service. But we made it."

"Were there rough times?"

"Is the sky blue?" He chuckled. "If you love each other…"

"We do. At least I think we do."

"Then it'll survive."

"Why does it hurt so much?"

"Can't have love without pain," Bobby said as he eased them onto the highway.

She sat back against the leather seat and trained her unseeing gaze out the window. Memories of her last week with Jake flooded her mind. *This must be what Cara and Grant had. How did they do it? Guess if they can last seven years, I can last a few months.*

When they reached the airport, Bobby put her luggage in the hands of the skycap then hugged her. "Good luck, kid. This is a tough business. Don't let them get to you. Make yourself heard. And keep a light burning for Jake. He's a good guy."

She nodded. "I'll try, Bobby. Thanks for everything."

When he drove away, a wave of loneliness washed over Gracie. Now she was truly on her own. *Isn't this what I wanted? What I wished for? My chance? Can I cut it? I'll find out.* She took a deep breath and walked through the doors, heading for her gate.

Chapter Twelve

Grace clicked open the lock and went into the big house on Benedict Canyon Drive. *Everything looks the same. But nothing is the same. I'm not the same.* She smiled as she dragged her heavy suitcases into her bedroom. *Cara had to load me up with new clothes for this venture. Now I can barely lift this!*

She turned up the heater on the pool then whipped out her cell to call Jake. *Oops! He's on stage!* She put it away and unpacked. Then she checked the house and called the security company to tell them she was there and would be staying.

Grace kicked off her shoes and padded into the kitchen to make a grocery list. After swishing her toes in the pool to determine if the water was warm enough, she stripped off her clothes and dove in. *Swimming alone. Against Cara's rules. I can handle it.*

Grace swam laps for twenty minutes. She climbed out, exhausted. Barely able to drag herself into the shower, she washed the chlorine off her body and fell into bed. Sleep engulfed her, driving all worries from her mind.

The next morning, she was up early and ready to rock. Dressed in linen pants and jacket plus a bright turquoise scoop neck, silk blouse, she headed out the door. When she turned on the SUV, butterflies invaded her stomach. *My first script conference! It's really happening. S*he typed the address of the office in the GPS, took a deep breath, and put the car in gear.

On the third floor of a modern low-rise office building just off Hollywood Boulevard, a pretty receptionist showed Grace into a swanky conference room. Off-white walls set off the huge mahogany table with a dozen comfortable swivel chairs hugging the edge. A nondescript, industrial rug in beige ran from wall to wall. Modern paintings with bright colors cheered up the cold room.

She was the first to arrive, so she pulled out a hard copy of the screenplay, a pen and notebook, leaving her laptop in its case.

When the door opened, Grace turned to face a young man, about twenty-six, not tall, nice looking, with brown hair and eyes.

He extended his hand. "Hi. I'm George Carpenter. Max Webster hired me to work with you."

"Is he coming?"

"He's in New York. He doesn't usually get involved in script work at this stage unless there's a problem."

Grace shook his hand and smiled. "Have you read the script?"

"I liked it very much. Great story, but the dialogue needs a little work."

"That's all?" She raised her eyebrows.

"Not really. We might have to shuffle a few scenes...writers don't usually like to hear about a ton of changes on their work right away. So I like to start small."

Grace laughed. "Give it to me straight, George. I can take it."

He turned on his computer, and they put their heads together for the next three hours. Grace tried to listen with an open mind. *How much do I let him change, and how much do I take a stand on keeping?* George was pleasant but insistent on some changes, and Grace's stomach did flip flops as she tried to figure out how to handle him. *When do I put my foot down?*

At noon, he invited Grace to lunch. "Come on. My treat. You've been really good about stuff. Time for a reward. I know a great little seafood restaurant in Long Beach. Do you like seafood?"

She climbed into his Corvette, and they drove to a cute restaurant called Fisherman's Cove. The head waiter showed them to a secluded table in an empty room. He gave George a knowing look, palmed the twenty buck tip, and left them alone. Grace slid into the booth and was surprised when George moved in next to her.

"Max didn't tell me you were so...lovely," he practically purred, as his gaze settled on her chest.

Grace unfolded her napkin as a knot formed in her stomach. *Please, God, not down this road again.* She picked up a menu. "What's good here? I'm starved."

"How about a drink first? They make a mean Cosmo."

"No alcohol when I'm working. Do you drink and work?"

"Hey, this is L.A., everyone does."

"Not me." She forced herself to look over the food choices. *Good move, Gracie. No alcohol.* She could feel heat from his thigh, pressing against hers. She tried inching away to the other side, but she was flush up against the wall. After taking a breath, she worked up her courage. "Would you mind moving to the right? I'm feeling a little crowded."

George lifted his eyebrows but moved a few inches away, breaking physical contact.

"The cold shrimp salad looks divine. And a mint iced tea works for me."

"Mint tea? Really?"

She nodded. The waiter approached, and George placed their order. He ordered a Cosmo and a steak for himself. The drinks arrived quickly.

Grace silently prayed the food service would be fast.

"Tell me about yourself, Grace. You're Cara Brewster's sister, right?"

"I am. Not much to tell. This is my first screenplay."

"I figured," George chuckled.

Heat traveled into Grace's cheeks at his comment. "I'm a hard worker, and I take direction well."

"That's what Gunther said."

At the sound of Gunther Quill's name, she stiffened. *Why did he mention Gunther? He's not producing this movie.* Grace took a gulp of her tea to bide time while figuring out what to do. *Get the facts.* "Gunther Quill?" she asked.

"Said he knows you…quite well."

"We've met."

George laughed, and Grace's pulse vibrated in her neck while her stomach squeezed. *Oh my God! Gunther told him!* Tears pricked at the back of her eyes, but she was determined not to give in. *No crying. Grow up!*

"Have you ever collaborated on a script before?" She shook her head. "Well, collaboration goes much better, smoother, and the end result is way better if the people writing together…uh…get together in a more personal way, too."

Shit! He's propositioning me! Damn you, Gunther Quill! Bastard! "What?" She raised her eyebrows and feigned an innocent look.

"You're very beautiful, Grace. We could have a lot of fun while we work on this script, if you'll simply…" The waiter appeared with their food, interrupting George.

Anger bubbled up inside Grace until she thought she'd explode, right in the restaurant. Her lips compressed into a thin line, she tried to smile at the server but couldn't. *Take it easy. Don't kill George. Stand up for yourself. You're the screenwriter.* The salad looked beautiful, but her appetite had gone south. "If you're suggesting I sleep with you to get the script done, forget it. Never. No way."

"I'm disappointed. Gunther told me—"

"I don't care what Gunther told you. He's a liar. I'm in a relationship, and even if I weren't, I'd never sleep with a colleague to get the job done. I'm not a hooker or a whore, George, and I resent your insinuations that I am."

George raised his palms to her. "Well, excuse me! Sorry. Gunther told me you were ripe for…game for…a good time. Guess I got it wrong."

"You sure did." Hunger broke through her ire. A smile of satisfaction tugged at her lips. To cover her triumph, Grace tore into the shrimp salad. *Hah! Spoke up! Take that, you asshat creep.*

They ate in silence for a while. "If you change your mind…" he began, slicing off a piece of steak.

"What would Max Webster say if he knew you propositioned me?"

"I assume Max is a sophisticated guy who knows how these things—"

"Max is a devoted family man. I don't think he'd like it at all."

His face grew several shades paler. "You're not going to tell him, are you?"

"Give me one good reason…"

"I need this job."

"Yeah? And I need a great screenplay. If you got where you are by sleeping with people, maybe you can't deliver."

"Oh, I can. I'm good. I'm very good. Have you seen a list of my credits?"

"Perhaps Max should've let me interview you before he hired you. I might have to tell him you won't do." She stared at him.

He began to sweat. "Please. I'm sorry. I won't do that again."

"And see that you stop spreading ugly rumors about me started by Gunther Quill."

"I will. I promise. My lips are sealed. Please don't get me fired."

"Time will tell. You'd better produce, George. Or you'll be replaced, like that!" She snapped her fingers.

They finished lunch with a minimum of conversation and returned to the conference room. The rest of the day was spent reading aloud, discussing, arguing, and rearranging scenes. There was no more talk of sexual collaboration. George was all business.

When Grace returned home with a bag of groceries, she toed off her shoes and poured herself a glass of wine. Sitting on the deck by the pool, she checked the time. *Damn! Eight o'clock in New York. Curtain's up.*

After making her dinner, reading the latest issue of *Celebs 'R Us* and the *LA Times,* she glanced at her watch. *Eleven o'clock in New York!* She dialed Jake's number and stretched out on the sofa.

Grace told Jake all about George.

"You told him *no* right?"

"Of course! How can you even ask?" She bolted upright.

"Just making sure."

"Faithful to you all the way. Besides, I don't do hook-ups. And George is definitely not my type...sleazy scumbag."

"If I was there, I'd punch him out. Bastard. Making a pass at my girl." She heard the anger in his voice.

"I handled him. In the afternoon, he was all business."

"I'm proud of you."

A broad smile spread across her face. "Really?"

"You're standing up for yourself, as you should."

"How was the show?"

"Fine. Good audience tonight. They got the jokes. What are you wearing?"

She quickly disrobed. "Uh...nothing?"

"Really?"

"Yep." She could hear his breath catch for a second.

"I can picture that. Hell, yeah. I can see you."

"What about you?"

"Boxers."

"Take 'em off."

"Aye, aye, captain." She heard him put the phone down. "Naked here."

"Good. That's the way I like you."

"Hey, that's my line."

Grace laughed.

"I wish you were here, Gracie. Miss you so much."

"Miss you, too."

"Work hard. Finish your script and come home to me."

Home, the way he says it. Sounds so wonderful. "I will," she whispered. "Love you, Jake."

"Love you back…more," he said. They both kissed into the mouthpiece and hung up.

Grace sighed as the ache in her heart pounded. "Work hard? I will, Jake. I will." She dragged herself to the bedroom and slipped under the sheet. Sleep came quickly.

* * * *

Once Grant's divorce was final, Cara set the date for their wedding. June fifteenth was reserved at Limoges. Grace found herself on the phone daily with Cara to discuss the menu, guest list, and what she should wear. The two sisters spoke so often, sometimes Grace had a hard time focusing on her script. But George cracked the whip and together they hammered out a workable screenplay that Max gave his approval to by the end of May.

Poised to call Jake and tell him she was coming back, her phone rang. She glanced at the display. It said Max Webster.

"Hi, Max. What's up?"

"Great job with George on the screenplay. Still have a couple of bumps, but we can work with the director on those."

"Good. Can I come back to New York now?"

"Not yet. I'm coming out there for casting meetings. We want you to be in on the process, Grace."

"How long will that take?"

"Couple of months, tops. If we're lucky. Negotiations and scheduling can be tricky."

Grace heaved a sigh.

"Something wrong, Gracie?"

"I was planning to return to the city. See Jake, Cara..."

"We're giving you some time off for Cara's wedding. Isn't that enough?"

"I guess."

"Don't you want to be involved in this?" She heard the note of irritation in his voice.

"Of course. Of course, I do. Max, please. This comes first. I get that."

"Good. Don't forget it."

"I won't. How much time for the wedding?"

"Figure two weeks should be enough."

"So when can I leave?"

"Hmm...I believe I have you booked on a flight at three this afternoon. It's eleven now, better hurry."

"Max! You're a doll! Thank you!" She heard him chuckle before she hung up. There was no time to call Jake. *I'll surprise him!* She laughed as she threw clothes into her suitcase. *Won't Cara be pleased?*

The flight seemed to take longer than usual. Grace squirmed in her seat, unable to sit still. Max had booked her first class. *Better not get used to this.* She drank champagne instead of napping. Word puzzles, books, magazines, newspapers—nothing held her attention for long. Goddard Towns, a well-known character actor, sat next to her, and his banter kept her entertained until they touched down.

Grace checked her watch. *Eleven forty-five. Go right to the apartment.* Grace patted her pocket as the cab wended its way through the New York City highways on route to the Upper West Side. She found her key and sat back, smiling, watching the sky light up as the nightlife shifted into high gear. *How surprised Jake is going to be!*

Once inside the building, Grace lugged her suitcase up the stairs, excitement flowing through her veins. *Just in time for bed!* Chuckling at the idea, she kept trudging upward, stair after stair, flight after flight. She'd forgotten how long it took to arrive on the third floor of this walk-up. She fitted the key in the lock and turned.

Opening the door, her gaze fell on a sight she never expected—a slinky brunette with her arms around Jake's neck.

* * * *

"What the hell?" Grace dropped her bag.

"Grace! What are you doing here?"

"Visiting you. But I can see you're busy." She turned to go but Jake broke free from the woman, grabbed her arm, and spun her around. He drew her into his embrace and hugged her tight. She pushed against his arms, but he wouldn't let go.

"Gracie, honey, I'm so glad to see you."

She stiffened. "Who's this?"

"I'm Traci. We go way back."

"Who?" When Jake loosened his grip, Grace finally stepped away and cast a jaundiced eye at the girl.

"Traci is my former girlfriend."

"The one who broke your heart? Who dumped you?"

Jake blushed and nodded.

"Oops. Sorry. Guess I wasn't supposed to tell the truth."

"I can explain," Jake started.

Grace scowled at Traci. "What are you doing here, and how long have you been here?"

"I just got here. Honestly…"

"Show didn't finish until ten thirty, Gracie…"

"I know. Go on," she snapped.

"I came to see Jake because…well, maybe I was hasty. I mean, maybe I made a mistake." Traci fidgeted with the hem of her shirt.

"Trying to get back together?"

"Yeah." She cast her gaze to the floor and shifted her weight.

"And what did he say?"

"I…"

"Shhhh…let her tell me!" Grace put her finger on his lips.

"He told me he had you, and he wasn't interested. Then he said a few unpleasant things…accused me of…well, returning because he's famous now and stuff…and Jared is out of work. But it's not true."

"Not true?" She cocked an eyebrow at the interloper.

"Honestly, Gracie, that's what I said…"

"It's okay, Jake. I believe you. What I mean is, I don't believe the part about her saying she didn't come back because you're famous. That's exactly why she came back."

A sullen, hostile look swept over Traci's face. "Who the hell are you to talk to me like that?"

"The woman who loves Jake."

"Oh?" She raised her eyebrows at Grace. "Then why was he alone when I came?" She shifted her weight and rested her hand on her hip.

"Because I was in California. I trust Jake." *Dear God, I do still trust him, don't I?*

"Big mistake."

"We have a pact."

"Honey, don't be naïve. He's a man and men cheat. You're a fool." Her lips curled into a snarl.

"Who's Jake's love now, you or me?"

"And who else did he screw while you were away?"

"No one," Jake piped up. "Grace and I talk every night. She knows I wouldn't cheat."

"You had him and tossed him out. Too bad. I think you should leave now," Grace said, holding the door open. Traci shot an imploring look at Jake, but all she received was a cold stare.

"Go, Traci," he said.

"Goodbye, Jake. It was fun."

"Goodbye. Good luck."

She stopped to kiss Jake on her way out.

"That's not a woman, that's a tiger." Traci turned and walked down the hall, her high heels tapping out a saucy rhythm on the marble floor.

"You do believe me, don't you, Grace?" His brow furrowed.

"Tell me all about it…don't leave anything out," she said, sinking down onto the sofa. Jake poured a glass of wine for them both then joined her and related the tale of the unexpected visitor from his past.

"You do believe me, don't you?"

"I do." She looked at him. With his hair hanging over his forehead and a concerned expression clouding his caramel-colored eyes, he looked more handsome than ever. He took her in his arms and kissed her long and deep.

"Are you here to stay?" He kept his arm around her.

"Nope. More meetings, casting stuff. Busy, busy." Grace snuggled into him.

"How long will you be here?"

"Through the wedding…two weeks." *God it feels good to touch him.*

"I'll take what I can get. You're staying with me, right?"

"If you want me."

"You have to ask?" He stroked her hair.

Another kiss heated up the lovers, who began to undress each other, slowly at first then frantically as their passion burned out of control. Jake barely got the bed pulled out before their bouncing made the springs squeak.

After they made love, Grace reached for her phone. "Must call Cara." Jake circled her wrist, stopping her before her fingers closed around the cell.

"Not tonight. Tomorrow. Tonight you're all mine." He kissed her neck.

"If you insist."

"I do. Come here." He pulled the covers down and slipped in first before bidding her to join him. Grace crawled up next to him and rested her head and hand on his chest. *Heaven.*

"I've missed you," she whispered.

"Me, too. I'm sorry about Traci."

"Already forgotten."

"Just us."

"Just us." A contented sigh sprang from her lips.

Jake turned out the light, and they drifted off to sleep woven together.

Chapter Thirteen

On her wedding day, Cara was a nervous wreck. She paced in the apartment. Grant had moved to a hotel the night before. Grace tried to calm her down.

"I've got a list, Carol Anne. Everything is checked off. Now you can relax."

"Relax? Relax, you say? I don't think so." Cara continued to pace.

"Everything is done. The sun is shining. The food will be great. The musicians are the best. Let's get you dressed."

"Now?"

"That's all that's left. Dressing you and me. And Jake's arrival." Grace took her sister by the hand and led her into the bedroom.

She took the pure white dress from the closet and lifted the lightweight plastic bag. A straight, knee-length sheath in white silk taffeta with an over layer of white silk chiffon looked beautiful even on the hanger. The neckline was a wide scoop with a row of two-inch ruffles all the way around. Sleeveless was the most flattering style. Grace held the gown while Cara shed her robe and stepped into it.

"Just let me zip this up." Grace pulled the zipper all the way from her sister's behind to mid-back. She closed the little hook and eye. "Grant's gonna have a helluva time getting this off you."

"Hooks and zippers never stopped him before," Cara snickered.

Grace placed the small headband covered with fresh gardenias and tiny pearls in her sister's hair and pulled down the short veil. "Omg, Cara!"

"What? What's wrong?"

"You look breathtaking!" Gracie's eyes watered. "If only mom could be here for this." They sank down on the bed. Try as they might, they couldn't contain all their tears and a few slipped out. Gracie handed her sister a tissue and took one for herself.

"Pookie, you look gorgeous, too." Cara remarked, eyeing the light turquoise silk empire-waisted dress that fell to Grace's knees. Hers was also sleeveless and had a square neckline with lace edging.

Grace fastened her mother's pearl choker around Cara's neck. The bride pulled a blue garter up her thigh. "I think I'm ready." The buzzer sounded. "That must be Jake and Bobby."

Jake gasped when he saw the Brewster sisters. "Wow, you two look…awesome. Unbelievable."

They grinned at him. Jake extended an arm to each lady, and they left the apartment. Grant had picked up Sarah, the flower girl dressed in a dress identical to Grace's, earlier in the day. Jake wore his tux as he was giving the bride away.

Bobby drove them as close as he could to Limoges, parked the car, and joined them, since he and Peg were invited guests. Grace leaned over and whispered to Cara, "We'll finally get to meet Bobby's wife!"

Jean Marc greeted them at the door. "All the guests are here, sipping champagne. There are seventy-five, non?"

"Oui, seventy-five. Thank you," Cara said, flashing him the blindingly brilliant smile that lit up movie screens across the country.

He escorted them to the room that Limoges reserved for private parties. The space had three walls of small panes of glass that looked out onto the gardens in Central Park. Pots of colorful geraniums had been placed outside and many arrangements of tulips, roses, and baby's breath were set up inside. It looked gorgeous and smelled divine.

Jean Marc delivered a flute of the bubbly to Cara, Grace, and Jake. Bobby had joined his wife and the other guests. Cara's hand shook as she tossed down her drink.

"You can't be nervous marrying Grant!" Grace was surprised at her sister's reaction.

"It's not about marrying Grant. It's about the performance. A wedding is like a show. What if something goes wrong? There's no director or stage manager here to handle it."

"I'm the director and stage manager rolled into one. If anything goes wrong, I'll fix it. I promise."

"What would I do without you, Pookie?"

"You gotta stop calling me that. I'm a professional screenwriter now."

A few lights flashed. Cara had agreed to let Tiffany Cowles and one of her photographers attend the wedding. But the photographer had to leave before the reception. Jean Marc interrupted their conversation. He handed bouquets to each lady—pink flowers for Cara, white for Grace.

"Everyone is here. We're ready to start."

Strains of Vivaldi's "Four Seasons" reached their ears as Sarah and Jane Hollings, Grant's sister and the other bridesmaid, joined them.

"Come on," the young girl said. Jean Marc took Sarah and Grace to the aisle. Jake offered his arm to Cara.

"Nervous?" he asked her.

"Terrified!" she whispered, slipping her hand through his arm.

"But it's just another performance." He placed his hand over hers.

"It's the rest of my life."

"Do you doubt Grant's the one? 'Cause I'll hold everyone back while you flee, if that's what you want."

"You're sweet." She cupped his face. "No, Grant's the one."

"So don't be nervous. Be happy."

She smiled broadly. "You're right." She took a deep breath, closed her fingers around his arm, and stood up straight.

"Ready?" he asked.

"Ready," she breathed.

Jake nodded to Jean Marc and the piano player began Mendelssohn's "Wedding March." Cara and Jake proceeded down the aisle slowly. Grace watched her sister's gaze connect with Grant's. He was grinning, his eyes wide. Gary Lawrence, Jane Hollings' live-in love, was the best man. Grace was barely able to blink back tears of joy at the look of happiness on Cara's face. *Maybe someday I'll have this, too.*

The ceremony and the receiving line passed in a blur for Grace. Jean Marc kept refilling her champagne glass, and she lost track of time. The string quartet was playing, and Cara and Grant were on the dance floor. Jake danced with Sarah and Gary with Jane.

Grace leaned against the wall. Suddenly a woman was beside her.

"It's nice to finally meet the Movie Maven," Tiffany Cowles purred.

Grace turned abruptly. "Tiffany?" The woman gave a nod. "Nice to meet you, too. Thank you for running the review of Jake's movie and for trying to stop Gunther Quill."

"No thanks necessary. Didn't mean to ruin your life, just wanted an exciting cover story."

When the dance was over, Tiffany rejoined her husband. Jake wandered over. "Been looking all over for you." He took her hand.

"We can dance the next one."

"Max Webster is here."

"Of course. Love Max."

"He gave me the news. Thank you so much. You're amazing," Jake said.

Grace blushed. "I don't know what you're talking about." She gazed at the floor.

"Total truth, remember?" He lifted her chin with his finger until their eyes met.

"Okay, okay, I know. Are you happy about it?" She chewed her lip.

"To have a part in your movie… Are you kidding?"

"You're perfect for it. Will Max give you the time off Broadway?"

"We're negotiating that now. He's joking that he has to negotiate with himself!"

She laughed. "He told me he was relieved to have one part cast already."

"Then we can be together," Jake said. "Come on." He led her around the corner, through a side door to a secluded alcove in the garden. He sat her down on a white, wrought iron bench. The metal was cold on the back of her legs, but the look on Jake's face was warm. He reached into his pocket and brought out a small, black velvet box.

Her hand flew to cover her mouth. *This can't be what I think it is, can it?*

Jake knelt down on one knee and opened it, revealing a three carat round cut diamond ring. "Gracie, I love you with all my heart. Will you marry me?"

Tears gushed forth, spilling down her cheeks. In a quick movement, Jake whipped out his handkerchief and shoved it into Grace's hands. She mopped up her cheeks before the wetness stained her dress.

"Geez, didn't think proposing would bring waterworks." Jake was crestfallen.

"Yes."

"What?" He looked up at her.

"I said *yes*. Isn't that what you wanted to hear?"

"You mean you *will* marry me?"

"Yes. How many times do I have to say it?"

Jake jumped up and pulled Gracie into his arms. A passionate kiss followed.

* * * *

Inside, Cara was looking for her sister.

"G, have you seen Gracie?"

He touched his finger to his lips and took her hand. Leading her around to the side of the room, he pointed at the young couple in the garden, locked in a loving embrace. The newlyweds paused, champagne glasses in hand, to watch the young lovers.

"I'd better eat carefully," Cara muttered, grinning.

"Why?" Grant asked.

"Looks like this dress is going to be needed again very soon."

Epilogue

On a plane to Los Angeles

When Grace found her good friend was flying west, she pleaded with the stewardess to allow them to sit together. Since the flight was light, there was an empty seat next to Gracie, and the switch was made. They were flying first class.

Once the seatbelt sign was off, champagne was served.

"Why back to L.A. so soon?" Gracie asked.

Dorrie's eyes glowed. "I've been hired to choreograph a new movie. The producer is paying for this first class seat. I couldn't afford it."

Grace's eyebrows shot up.

"Yep! *Hustle and Dance*, the Broadway musical, is being made into a movie. Chaz Duncan is going to star in it, too."

"That's fabulous!"

"If the movie is successful, they're planning a miniseries and then a regular TV series."

"Wow! You'll make a ton of money. I didn't know you did choreography."

"I started after I broke my ankle. I had to kiss my dance career goodbye."

"A silver lining to a terrible cloud."

Dorrie nodded just as they were interrupted to place their order for dinner. Both women requested the chicken Cordon Bleu.

"How awful to lose your career like that."

"My star was on the rise, great role in a movie, hot producer fiancé. I was living my dream."

"And then?" Grace coaxed.

"I couldn't dance anymore. The part in my second movie went to someone else, and my fiancé went south, too. It's ironic, I broke my ankle falling down the stairs of his beach house."

"Oh my God! What a bastard!"

"Yeah. I've missed dancing. I give dance and yoga lessons to be doing what I love, but I barely scrape by. The dance contest brought some important people…thanks to you and Jake."

Their meals arrived, and the hungry women tucked into their food.

"This new job'll bring you big bucks?" Grace asked between bites.

"I hope. So much depends on other people. I mean, the movie pays well, but the other stuff…have to wait and see."

"Your fiancé walked out on you during your biggest crisis?" Grace shook her head.

"It's been three years. I'm finally over it." Dorrie speared a cooked carrot with her fork.

"You're so beautiful. I'd think you'd have your pick, Dorrie. Why'd you choose him?"

"I was pretty full of myself five years ago. I walked away from three terrific men in New York to come to L.A. to end up with him. Maybe I was hasty." Dorrie ran her fingers through her dark auburn locks.

"Three guys?"

"Yeah. Still wonder if I had had one more day with each of them, would it have made a difference?"

"And yet you ended up with this creep?"

Dorrie chuckled and took another sip of champagne. "My first movie was a big success. Success attracts all kinds of bloodsuckers."

Grace thought of George for a second. "Well said. Who is this lowlife producer?"

"You might have heard of him—Gunther Quill?"

Grace spit out the champagne she had been drinking. "Who?"

"Gunther Quill. We were engaged for a year. Guess you've heard of him."

"He has quite a reputation," Grace sensed blood rushing to her face.

"Well deserved, too. He's slime."

They continued to eat in silence for a bit. Dorrie noticed Grace's ring.

"Let me guess–engaged to Jake?"

Grace nodded and smiled.

"You two make a great pair. He's smart to snap you up."

"Thanks. What about you? On the verge of great success. Anyone special in the picture?"

Dorrie shook her head. "Haven't met anyone good. I've been working so hard to get this chance, and now with no one to share it… makes it a little…empty."

"What are you gonna do about it?"

The ride got a little bumpy, and the seatbelt sign flashed on right away. The stewardess came by to take their trays and refill their champagne glasses.

"I have to go back to New York for three weeks this summer to film a dance sequence in Central Park for the movie."

"Oh?" Grace lifted her eyebrows.

"Yeah. I'm tacking on some vacation time, too."

"Are you going to look up…?"

"You got it. I'm going to have my one more day with each of them."

"That's so cool, Dorrie. I hope you find the right guy."

Dorrie raised her glass to make a toast. "Love, this is your last chance!"

The women clinked glasses. After they drained the bubbly, a ding from Dorrie's cell phone sounded.

"Text," she explained to Grace. Dorrie took out her phone and opened the message.

> *We need to talk. My car is coming for you at the airport.*
> *Gunther*

THE END

About the Author

Jean Joachim, wife and mother of two sons, is owned by a rescued pug, named Homer. She'd been writing non-fiction for what seemed like forever until she got up the nerve to try fiction. It was love. Now she spends her days in New York City in the company of her family, her characters, a cup of tea and a secret stash of black licorice.

OTHER BOOKS BY JEAN JOACHIM:

Now and Forever 1, A Love Story

Now and Forever 1, the Book of Danny

Now and Forever 3, Blind Love

The Renovated Heart

Under the Midnight Moon

Love Lost & Found (with Ben Tanner)

If I Loved You (Hollywood Hearts)

Red Carpet Romance (Hollywood Hearts)

Memories of Love (Hollywood Hearts)

Call of Duty (anthology)

Secret Cravings Publishing
www.secretcravingspublishing.com

Made in the USA
Charleston, SC
24 September 2013